Debbie

John Benton

NEW HOPE
BOOKS

Fleming H. Revell Company
Old Tappan, New Jersey

ISBN: 0-8007-8398-0
A New Hope Book
Copyright © 1981 by John Benton
All rights reserved
Printed in the United States of America
This is an original New Hope Book, published by
New Hope Books, a division of Fleming H. Revell
Company, Old Tappan, New Jersey

To Stephany Haas
whose great enthusiasm and
untiring efforts
reach down to many
a fallen girl like Debbie.

1 I gave the judge my best smile—the one I always used to get out of a jam.

Nothing. That old prune-face probably never smiled in his life, anyway. Besides, with the newspapers full of campus riots and anti-Vietnam demonstrations, chances were that old law-and-order would make it rough on any teenager brought before him—even a fourteen-year-old!

Well, maybe Dad was here. I glanced back. Sure enough, there was good old Dad in the third row. I guess for an adopted kid, I didn't have too many problems with him. He caught my eye and smiled. Good! He's probably been talking to the social-service workers. Everything was going to be okay—even with old prune-face on the bench.

"Young lady, look this way, please," the judge ordered.

I quickly turned, once again trying my most beguiling smile.

"That'll be enough of that," he said, his forehead creased in one of the worst frowns I had ever seen. "This is a very serious matter we have before us."

Serious? Ha! I was caught shoplifting a pair of jeans. Why did judges and courts and social workers and store owners have to make such a big deal over such a little thing?

"Do you go to school?" the judge asked.

"Yeah, I go to school," I answered nonchalantly. "I mean, sometimes."

"How often?" he persisted. "Five days a week, three days a week, one day a week? How often?"

Why all these questions about school? I wished he'd hurry up and get this ordeal over with and stop asking so many silly questions.

One of the things bothering me about this line of questioning was that my school attendance wasn't the best. But I figured I'd better lie in a situation like this. He wouldn't let me off if he thought I skipped school all the time. So I said, "Oh, I go to school almost every day. I mean, I really love school, Mr. Judge. I know it's good for me."

The judge let out a sarcastic, "Ha!" Then he added, "I've had hundreds of young people in this courtroom. They have been involved in all kinds of crimes, and I have yet to find one who really loves school. So tell me again, young lady, do you *really* love school?"

That should have been my clue. Right then and there I should have leveled with him. But not Debbie Carter. Oh, no! I never could admit getting caught in a lie.

"Mr. Judge," I answered indignantly, "like I told you, I really do love school. My father is sitting in this courtroom. Why don't you ask him?" I turned and pointed at my dad.

The judge called my father to the bench. "Mr. Carter, does your daughter really love school?"

I caught my breath. What would happen if Dad told the truth? He knew about my attendance record. In fact, one of the reasons I had never worried much about it was that he didn't seem to think it was all that important.

Dad hesitated. The whole courtroom hushed, and everyone's attention was riveted on my dad. "Yes,

Your Honor," he said, "I think my daughter really does love school."

You can believe I breathed a sigh of relief. Good old Dad. Always lying—like me and for me.

"I don't believe you," the judge announced matter-of-factly.

Dad's face turned ashen. The silence in the courtroom became a low buzz, and the judge banged his gavel down, ordering, "Silence!"

I either didn't hear that, or I was already on my feet yelling, "For crying out loud, Mr. Judge. You just heard my father. Maybe you don't trust teenagers, but can't you take my father's word for it?"

He banged his gavel again and ordered, "Sit down!" Then he went on, "Before considering your sentence, young lady, there is a procedure this court always follows. We got your attendance record from your principal. And, young lady, you have missed a lot of school. Your grades are very poor, and it's a sad thing that in this courtroom your father would lie for you. You are in serious trouble!"

By this time Dad had slunk to the back of the courtroom. I couldn't count on any more help from him!

The tone of the judge's voice scared me to death. If I was going to get out of this one, it would take some kind of a miracle—and I didn't believe in miracles. I tried my smile again, but I couldn't even force it onto my lips. I guess I had always known that someday my lying was going to do me in.

He banged his gavel again, cleared his throat, and announced, "In view of these circumstances, I have no choice but to sentence you to six months in the Titusville Training School for Girls."

I gasped in shock. "What? What did you say?"

Without answering he slammed his gavel down again and said, "Next case."

I screamed an obscenity at him. Two guards moved toward me and grabbed my arms. I struggled and looked back for my dad—only to see his back as he went out the door. Now I really felt all alone.

I screamed again, and one of the guards clamped his big hand over my mouth to stifle my voice. I reacted in the only way I knew—by biting his hand. Then he screamed and yelled, "Stop that, or I'm going to throw some handcuffs on you!"

I cursed again. The two guards lifted me by my arms, opened a door, and pushed me out into the hallway. They dragged me to an office, pushed me inside, and threw me into a chair. I screamed again, and once again that big hand was clamped over my mouth—only this time he dug his fingernails into my cheek. "Shut up!" he yelled, "or I'm going to rip that mouth right off your face!"

He was hurting me so much that I screamed again, but his hand prevented any noise from escaping. I forced my mouth open to bite. That's when he grabbed my nose and began to twist it. The pain was excruciating. "Shut up!" he yelled again.

I was no match for these two big lugs. I'd better calm down. But I still couldn't believe I was headed for Titusville!

Some of the girls I hung around with had been sent up there. They said it really was like a penitentiary. The matrons were really mean, and you couldn't do a thing. And no boys.

Just then the office door opened, and there stood Barb Cortier with her hands on her hips. "For crying out loud, Debbie," she remonstrated, "why didn't you keep your mouth shut?"

Mrs. Cortier worked for the court, and I remember her interviewing me after I had admitted that I took those jeans. She seemed so nice, so understanding, during that interview. But now, obviously, she was thoroughly disgusted with me.

"You dumb nut, Debbie," she went on. "You had a good chance to go free, and you blew it. I couldn't believe what I was hearing when I listened to you lie to the judge and then react the way you did to his sentence."

"What do you mean, react? How many years have you spent in the Titusville Training School for Girls?"

"Well, I haven't spent any, thank goodness. But I can tell you one thing. If you had kept your cool, things might have been different."

"What do you mean, keep my cool? I wasn't about to let them take me away calmly to that penitentiary!"

"That's exactly what I'm talking about, Debbie. You had a good chance for a suspended sentence. In fact, in my report I recommended a suspended sentence to the judge. Let me tell you something else, Debbie. I've been working in this court for many years, and I've seen girls with more serious crimes than yours get off with suspended sentences. Judge Holzer is really a wonderful man, but he demands the truth. If you had leveled with him about school, and if your dumb father had been honest, and if you had kept your big mouth shut, you would have walked out of that courtroom free as a bird. But you blew it!"

I could hardly fathom what she was telling me. Me and my big mouth! And my dumb father. If only he had told the truth, maybe things would have been different. But I never had been able to trust him to tell the truth about anything. Besides, he never could understand me. Oh, he let me do whatever I wanted, and I guess he thought he was really being good to me. But even then I knew that wasn't what I really needed in a parent.

"Debbie," Mrs. Cortier went on, "I was the one who contacted your school. I knew your record there, but some of the people at school said they thought you were a girl with tremendous potential. I really think you could have had another chance; but now you've blown it!"

"Please, please, Mrs. Cortier, please give me another chance," I begged. "I mean, I didn't really mean that outburst. I was nervous, and you know how that is. I said the wrong thing. My mouth has gotten me in so much trouble."

"Well, it's too late now. I'm in the process of making arrangements to send you upstate to Titusville."

"But, Mrs. Cortier, don't you know what that's going to do to me? I know all about Titusville. Some of my friends have been there, and let me tell you, when they got out, they were professionals in crime. Some of them went into prostitution. Some learned how to pick locks and got into burglary. Some even had made elaborate plans to rob banks! I mean, after those girls came back from Titusville, it was like they had graduated with a degree in crime. Professional criminals—that's what Titusville turns out."

I had tried to paint the picture as bleak as possible, and I knew I had her coming my way, for she just stared past me at the blank wall.

"Mrs. Cortier," I begged again, "please believe me. Titusville isn't the place for a girl who has stolen a pair of jeans. It'll make a hardened criminal out of me!"

All the pent-up emotion broke within me, and I began to sob like the end of the world had come.

She still didn't say anything, but she came over and tenderly put her arm around my shoulder.

I turned and looked up into her face and asked through my tears, "I suppose you investigated my family, didn't you?"

She nodded.

"And I suppose you found out I'm adopted, didn't you?"

She nodded again.

"But did you find out that it's been hell-on-earth for me living with that family? I've been haunted, since the day I knew I was adopted, to try to find out who my real parents were. But my adopted parents thought it was all foolishness. Why, they even made up stories that my mother was a junkie and my father a criminal. Then they would tell me how lucky I was to get to live with them.

"But it was just the opposite. You see, my adopted father never could hold a job very long. He's been fired more often than I can remember because of his dishonesty. He has always lied and cheated. In fact, he seemed more pleased with me when I lied than when I told the truth. I've seen him beat my adopted mother time after time when he came home drunk.

"And my adopted mother wasn't much better. She never would claim me as her daughter. She always referred to me as her adopted daughter. Every time she said that word *adopted,* I would cringe on the inside.

"I don't think she ever wanted me. She gave in to the adoption because that was what her husband wanted. She never treated me like a mother ought to treat a daughter."

Mrs. Cortier stood there taking it all in. I knew she had probably heard sob stories like this hundreds of times, but it seemed like my only hope to get out of going to Titusville. And this time I really was telling the truth!

"Now, Mrs. Cortier," I pleaded, "please, please forgive me. I know I shouldn't have said what I did. I beg of you, I mean, I really beg of you, please give me one more chance. So help me, I know that if I'm sent to that penitentiary, all the bitterness and rebellion that I have on the inside are going to make me hate society like I've never hated it before. I know how weak I am. I won't be able to resist those girls up there with their wicked ways. Six months from now when I get out of Titusville, I know I'll just go into a life of crime. Eventually you know what will become of me. I'll be put behind bars for years!"

She was still staring at the wall. So I said, "Is that what you really want to become of me?"

Finally she looked me in the eyes. "Wait here," she said. "I'll be right back."

Wait here? Where could I go? Those two guards were still sitting there watching me.

"That was quite a speech, kid," one of them volunteered when Mrs. Cortier left the office. "Where did you learn that one?"

I glared at him. "Keep your big mouth shut!" I retorted. "I meant every word of it."

I guess I really didn't mean *every* word of it, but most of it I did. At this point I was ready to try anything to save my skin. I sure didn't want to give those guards the impression that I had been lying, or they might go to the judge and tell him not to believe what I said.

The judge! Was that who Mrs. Cortier went to see? Was there somehow still a chance that the judge would change his mind and give me a suspended sentence? Or had Mrs. Cortier heard that same kind of story from so many girls that she just couldn't take it any more and had gone to make the arrangements to send me to Titusville.

One of the guards broke into my thoughts. "Listen, kid," he told me, "we've handled thousands of smart alecks like you. Believe me, you're going to learn your lesson when you get up to Titusville. You'll swear to high heaven that you'll never commit another crime as long as you live. Once they lock you in there, kid, you begin to think about what freedom really is. That place will scare you to death, and you'll think twice about doing anything that'll get you back in the slammer again. For a lot of kids, it's the best thing that could ever happen to them."

"Sir," I said, trying to hold back my sarcasm, "how many years have you spent in Titusville?"

He glared at me. "Don't be so dumb, kid. Obviously, I've never been there. It's for girls! It's the smart alecks like you and these rotten, rioting college kids who make this world such a terrible place. They ought to lock up all the thieves and murderers and junkies and draft dodgers and throw the keys away. That would teach all this criminal element a thing or two and make this world a safer place."

I felt my fist tighten. Oh how I wanted to belt that guard in the mouth. He acted so big and know-it-all with that uniform on. He really had no understanding of the problems that kids like me had. And I despised him for being so totally lacking in understanding.

Fortunately the door opened just then, and Mrs. Cortier returned with the message: "The judge wants to see you again."

One of the guards spit on the floor in disgust. My heart began to beat faster. Was there really hope for me? Or was the judge going to add to my sentence because of my outburst in the courtroom? Oh, no! I hadn't even thought of that possibility!

Mrs. Cortier took me by the arm and led me down the hall. In another office we saw a secretary sitting at a desk. Mrs. Cortier said to her, "Judge Holzer wanted to see Debbie Carter again."

"He's in his chambers," the secretary said. "You may go right in."

I followed Mrs. Cortier to the next door. She knocked lightly on it, and I heard a familiar voice respond, "Come in."

She opened the door, and there sat Judge Holzer behind a huge mahogany desk. Volume upon volume of law books lined shelves that stretched clear up to the ceiling. Somehow I felt very small as I entered.

Judge Holzer stood and motioned us to some chairs. I thought about smiling, but since that didn't work last time, I decided against it. This time I wasn't going to speak unless I was spoken to; and this time I was going to tell the truth. So when he motioned us to the two chairs in front of his desk, I sat down immediately. Whatever the judge wanted, he was sure going to get it from me!

I noticed my knees knocking together. I was scared to death. Sitting across that huge desk was a man I didn't know—but a man who held my future in his hands. He could suspend my sentence or send me away for an even longer time. This time I had to act like a real lady.

"Mrs. Cortier has come back to me and asked me to reconsider your sentence of six months at the Titusville Training School for Girls," Judge Holzer started. "We've had substantial discussions in the past about the benefits of Titusville. In some cases, I believe it is where girls like you should go. It teaches them a profound lesson."

I started to protest that I would come out of Titusville a hardened criminal, but at least I had learned one lesson. I knew better than to play games with this judge. I got trapped into lying about school, so I just bit my lip.

"I also understand that for some girls Titusville becomes the wrong kind of training school," the judge went on. "Some girls are worse when they come out. I recognize that."

The judge did sound reasonable. At least he knew the bad points about Titusville.

"And, Debbie Carter, your stealing those jeans is not really the point of the discussion. I have a responsibility in my court to hand out sentences for violations of the law. Those sentences are to be punitive, trying to deter you from further crime. Sometimes girls like you will stop with just a warning. Others stop if I send them to Titusville. Others never ever stop. What category do you fit?"

I couldn't believe what I said next. I said, "I think you should send me to Titusville."

After I said it, a huge lump formed in my throat, and I started to cry. It embarrassed me, but I couldn't control myself.

Mrs. Cortier put her hand on my arm and patted it.

I cried for a few minutes, then I slowly raised my head and looked at the judge. "Mr. Judge," I said, "I feel absolutely worthless. I know no one really cares what happens to me. I guess you know I've been adopted, and my adopted parents don't really care what happens to me.

"I have very few friends at school. And, yes, it's the truth, I rarely go to school. My adopted parents told me my real dad was a criminal and my real mom was a junkie, and I guess I'm going to end up just like them. I steal, I cheat, and sometimes I use drugs. But, Mr. Judge, there's something about me that I just can't help what I do. Yes, I think you ought to send me away to Titusville. I think that's where I must belong."

This was no game now. I was sick and tired of fighting the system and trying to go right when I knew I couldn't. I didn't want to go back home, where it was hell. I didn't want to go back to school, where it was so hard for me. I didn't want to be out on the street, where my friends were, who were always up to no good. Maybe if I got locked away in Titusville, it really would be the best thing for me. After all, where else could I go?

Going back to the Bay Ridge section of Brooklyn was like going back to hell. It seemed that all my friends were stealing, and some of them were becoming junkies. With my folks on welfare, we had very little with which to meet the necessities of life. It didn't look as though they would ever get out of the welfare trap. I guess that's what got me started in stealing. From the little I'd experimented, I knew that drugs brought me some temporary relief, but they weren't the way out.

I was fourteen then, but as I sat across from the

judge and thought about my life, I felt like an old lady.

"Debbie, come over here for a minute," Judge Holzer said as he stood.

I rose from my chair obediently and walked over behind his desk and stood next to him.

"I think I know what you need," he said. Then he threw his arms wide out. I jumped back. He was going to hit me!

With his arms still outstretched, he smiled and said, "Don't be afraid. My wife, Lois, and I have eight children. Most of them are grown now, and they all haven't been angels. But, thank God, none of them have had to appear before a judge. Oh, they did get into some trouble; but when they did, there was something that Lois and I always did. Here, I want to show you."

What in the world was this judge driving at? Certainly he wasn't going to take me over his knee and spank me. Or was he?

He took a step toward me with his arms still outstretched. I stood there straight as a rod. If he was going to spank me, so help me, I wasn't going to cry.

Just then his two big arms went around my shoulders, and he gently drew me up to himself and squeezed me tight. It was the most beautiful hug I had ever experienced in all my life!

I just couldn't help it, and once again the tears came. I'd rarely ever had anyone hug me, and I had never felt a hug like that one in all my life. Sometimes I'd stay overnight with my girl friends, and occasionally I'd see their fathers hug them. I secretly wished I had a father like that—one who knew how to hug. And with love.

I let my head fall onto the judge's shoulder as the

tears kept coming. He began to pat my back gently. Before I knew what I was doing, I half-raised my arms and began to hug the judge. Then I squeezed tight.

"Now, doesn't that feel good?" he asked me.

"Yes," I said between sobs, "that *does* feel good."

The judge pulled my chin up to where he was looking right into my eyes. "I've found that giving a child a loving, fatherly hug can cure the worst kind of behavior in anybody," he said. "Kids today are starved to know that somebody really loves them."

"Mr. Judge, nobody loves me," I sobbed.

He reached over and threw his arms around me again. "Debbie, you'll never have to say those words again. From this day on I want you to know that there are two people who really love you. Even three."

"Three people?" I asked. "Mr. Judge, there's nobody—I mean, nobody—in the whole wide world who loves me."

He smiled. "Let me tell you the first one who loves you is me," he said.

"But you're a judge," I remonstrated. "You can't say something like that!"

"Who said so?" he asked. "I did just say it, and I really mean it. If you turn into the worst criminal the world has ever known, I will still love you, Debbie. And there's someone else who loves you too."

I turned toward Mrs. Cortier. "Do you love me too?" I asked.

"I sure do!" she responded, her eyes shining with tears.

"And there's someone else who really loves you," Judge Holzer continued.

"Who's that?"

"Jesus loves you."

Well, I guess I must have thought the whole thing was a dream about that point. A few minutes ago in the courtroom, I was faced with a horrible future. Now I was in the judge's chambers, and the man I had referred to as old prune-face was telling me he loved me, and Mrs. Cortier said she loved me. Then the judge said that Jesus loved me. How in the world could a judge say something like that?

"Did you know Jesus loves you?" he asked.

I looked at him in surprise. "What did you say?" I asked.

He repeated the question.

"But, Mr. Judge, judges aren't supposed to say things like that."

He smiled broadly. "Well," he said, "I just said it. And it's just as true as my saying that I love you."

This was almost too much for me. Now I could face Titusville with a little different perspective. The judge loved me; Mrs. Cortier loved me; and Jesus loved me.

The judge led me back to the chair and then took his seat across from us. He leaned across that huge desk and said, "Now, Debbie, this is what I'm going to do. Mrs. Cortier and I have discussed your case again. After talking to you, I think it would be best if I didn't send you to Titusville. I think for you it would be the wrong decision. However, it will be necessary for us to make you a ward of the court and try to place you with another family. We're going to look for very special foster parents—people who can bring out the potential that I think is in you. I think your future and your outlook will change if you are in the right environment. At least we're going to pray that way."

This whole experience in the judge's chambers was too overwhelming for me to say anything. I was ready to agree to whatever he thought would be best for me.

But before long I found out that it was going to take more than new parents to change the course of my life.

2

The next two years were the best I had ever known. The court placed me with the Greens. They had six children of their own and really understood the problems of teenagers. I thoroughly enjoyed those two years on their farm in upstate New York. I was loved, disciplined, and encouraged to reach my potential.

As a child I had always dreamed of having my own horse, and that's just what happened on their farm. I learned to ride and to groom it and care for it. I really felt free as we galloped across the fields.

Of course, it wasn't all play. Every member of the family was expected to pull his or her own weight, and I was no exception. I learned to plow with a tractor, to milk the cows, to weed a garden. I was even getting so I could tell the good plants—the tomatoes and beans and peas—from the weeds. Quite a change from the asphalt jungle of Brooklyn!

During those two years I had almost no contact with my adopted parents. The Greens never did say much, but I heard in a roundabout way that they had become bums. My adopted father was an alcoholic now, and my mother had left him. I guess she had run off with some other man. Frankly, I felt good to be free of both of them. I never had been close to them. Besides, Mom and Dad Green were supplying all I needed in parents. I really learned to love both of them.

One night we gathered around the supper table for another of Mom Green's fabulous meals. Dad Green had gone into town for some supplies, but for some reason he was late for supper. That wasn't like him at all.

We went ahead and ate anyway. Mom said she was sure he would be along any minute.

Well, we got to our dessert, and still no Dad Green. I glanced over at Mom, and I could read the worry lines on her face. I knew that usually Dad would call if he was going to be late.

We finished dessert, washed the dishes, and turned on the TV. But I don't think anybody was really watching it. We were all getting worried now.

After what seemed like an eternity, we saw the lights of a car pulling down the long driveway. Mom Green rushed to the door. "I don't know who it is," she said, "but it certainly isn't Dad. That's not his car."

I went and stood beside her and peered out into the darkness. As the car got closer, I could make out the silhouette of lights and a siren on the top. It was the New York State Police!

What in the world did they want? Certainly they weren't coming after me, were they? For the last two years I hadn't broken any laws that I knew of. I certainly hadn't stolen any more jeans, and I sure didn't want the courts taking me away from here.

The officers drove up as close as they could and then walked to the door. "Are you Mrs. Green?" one of them asked.

"Yes, I am," Mom nervously replied.

"We are very sorry, Mrs. Green, but your husband was involved in a serious automobile accident."

"No! No!" she screamed. "It can't be true! Is he . . . ? Is he . . . ?"

The two officers gently took her arm and led her inside to a chair. "I'm sorry, Mrs. Green," one of them said, "but he was dead at the scene. We think he was killed instantly."

With that, Mom just went to pieces. All their other children, of course, were right there and heard the news. Everyone began to sob and cry. Even those big, tough cops had tears in their eyes. I couldn't help but wonder why something like this had to happen to such a wonderful man.

Mom was asking how it happened. The officers explained that a drunken driver, traveling at a high rate of speed, had plowed head on into Dad's car. The drunken driver lived. He was in the hospital, but not seriously injured. And Dad was dead.

As soon as the officer mentioned a drunken driver, I couldn't help but think of the bitterness I had in my heart toward my adopted father. Alcohol was so devastating! And now it had taken another innocent life —this time of a fine man whom I had come to love as a father.

The officers suggested Mom call some neighbors and the minister. They came right over. The minister had prayer with us; he seemed so helpful and understanding.

The next few days all of us were going around in a fog. There was such a vacuum without Dad around. The neighbors, bless them, helped with the chores. Everybody pitched in to do what they could.

But I started to worry about my status with the family. I knew the Greens never had a lot of money, and I wondered how Mom Green would be able to maintain the house for herself and her six children. I was obviously an added burden.

About a month later the people from the social service department came to visit. First they had a long talk with Mom Green. Then they invited me to join them.

I guess I knew what was coming. Mom Green was having a real struggle, they told me. Dad didn't have much insurance, and she had to find ways to cut her expenses. I came to understand that I was definitely a liability.

One social worker suggested I be placed with another family. "Debbie," she told me, "I'm sure we can find another home like this one."

"No way!" I responded. "No one could ever replace Mom and Dad Green."

"Now, now, Debbie, you're just a little upset," the social worker said. "I'm sure we can work out something that will be very satisfactory for everybody concerned."

I didn't want to hurt Mom Green, but I couldn't sit there and listen to that social worker say that.

"That's what you think!" I retorted. "I know quite a little bit about foster homes. Before coming here I ended up with a couple of alcoholics. They were the worst. Good foster parents are almost impossible to find, and you know that's the truth."

The social worker didn't respond. She just stared past me. She really knew that good foster parents were one in a million. I was just lucky to end up with the Greens.

We didn't settle anything at that moment, and when the social workers left, Mom Green put her arms around me and hugged me tenderly.

"Oh, Debbie, Debbie," she cried. "I just don't know if I can take your leaving our family. You are so much like my own now. You were so rebellious when you came, but you have become so different. Yet, I'm at my wit's end to know what to do. Honestly, honey, I don't want you to leave. I'm willing to try to work things out a little longer, but the social workers told me they thought it would be best. They're trying to be sympathetic and understanding about my living on a limited income now that Dad's gone. They're worried that it wouldn't be good for you or for the other children. I really hope you can understand." Her voice trailed off, and she hugged me and patted me so lovingly.

My heart was breaking, but I knew I had to be brave for Mom's benefit. So I said, "Mom, don't worry about it. I'm sure I'm going to be all right." Then I rushed away so she wouldn't see the tears that started to form.

That night in my room, I began laying my plans. I was sixteen now. I'd try to make it on my own rather than get with some family who would see me only as a burden and wouldn't even attempt to understand a mixed-up teenager.

I wrestled and wrestled with the problem and possible solutions until about two in the morning. Then I made up my mind.

I slipped out of bed, put my jeans and sweat shirt on, slipped on a pair of sneakers, packed a few necessities in a duffel bag, and quietly slipped out of the house. If I had to leave the Greens, then I'd be the one to decide where I was going. I wasn't willing to leave that choice to social workers.

But where could I go? The only place I really knew was New York City. Maybe some of my old girl friends there would help me. I guess I really didn't expect that, but it was one way of rationalizing my decision.

As I hiked across the farm, I thought of all those good times I was leaving behind. And I kept asking, over and over again, Why did Dad Green have to die? He was such a good man. But he did die, and my world had come to an end. It was about three miles from the farm to where the highway led to New York City. Through fields and woods I pushed my way along, stumbling in the dark and wondering if I shouldn't go back to Mom Green—or if I should have at least left her a note so she wouldn't worry about me.

But there was no time for looking back now. Just ahead was the highway—my road to a new life on my own, with no one telling me what to do or where to go. Now I would really be free.

No sooner had I hit the shoulder of the highway than I looked up the road and saw a big semitrailer barreling in my direction. I stuck out my thumb and immediately heard the whooshing of his air brakes. What luck! A ride already!

He pulled onto the shoulder, and I ran to the cab. That first step up looked mountainous, but I struggled up. He smiled as I opened the door and climbed in. "Hey, young girl," he said, "what in the world are you doing out so late on a road like this?"

Obviously I wasn't about to tell him I was running away. I had to think of something quick. So I said, "And you, Mr. Good-Looking, don't you know you're breaking the law by picking up a hitchhiker?"

He laughed easily. "Okay, kid, I won't ask any questions if you won't ask any questions." With that he steered the semi back onto the highway and slowly begain gaining momentum. But he also kept glancing in my direction.

"How far you going?" he asked.

"How far you going?" I countered.

"New York City," he responded. "Actually I'm running about six hours late. I should have been in by ten last evening, but I had trouble with a clogged diesel line up in Binghamton. But I'll get there."

"Hey, man, that's great!" I told him. New York City is where I'm headed. So I'm kind of glad you had that problem!"

He chuckled but didn't say anything. Yet I noticed him looking me over. The thing I feared most was probably on his mind. I knew all truck drivers weren't the same, but I also knew that some of them had dirty thoughts when they picked up a young girl. I decided I'd better defuse the situation right away.

"Are you married?" I asked.

"Hey, little thing, you trying to date me or something?"

Wrong question! "I mean, you look like a happily married man with a wife and some great kids. That's the reason I asked. What's wrong with a question like that?"

"Nothing, I guess," he responded. "But to tell you the truth, I'm divorced and free as a bird. My old lady ran around on me while I was out on trips. One time I got home a day early and caught her. That was it. No woman's going to cheat on me!"

I worried about the fact that he was divorced. But at least he despised cheating. I felt a little safer about that.

"What you going to do in New York City?" he asked.

"Oh, just some sight-seeing. I'm really from Ohio, and I'm making my way across the country. I got a ride with a guy all the way to near where you picked me up. He said I could spend the night with him in a motel, but no way was I going to do that. So my alternative was to be let out on that deserted stretch of highway in the wee hours of the morning. I was hoping some nice guy would come along and take pity on me, and sure enough, you did!"

"Oh, I see. For a minute there I thought maybe you were running away—maybe from a farm in upstate New York." Then he chuckled.

I didn't respond. I sure didn't intend to tell him anything about myself.

He drove on, and for about an hour both of us simply stared straight ahead. I was beginning to feel drowsy when he said, "I want to stop up here for coffee. But, kid, let's you and me get something straight before I stop. I'm going to be kind to you, and we'll walk in there together. I'll probably meet some buddies of mine in there, and as far as you and I are concerned, you're my daughter. Understand? Especially if a state cop happens to come in. I'm not about to get busted for picking up a delinquent. Now, you willing to play the game?"

"Of course I'll play your little game. But just between you and me, buddy, I'm not admitting to anything. I'm going to stick by my story of coming from Ohio. If you can lie, I can lie too. As far as you're concerned," I said as I pointed my finger at him, "I'm your daughter. But as far as I'm concerned, I'm from Ohio. You understand?"

He nodded. "Okay, kid, what's your name?"

It didn't seem too smart to give him my real name. After all, maybe Mom Green had already discovered

I had split and had called the police. So I said, "Susie Smith."

You should have heard him hee-haw! "Come off it, you dummy! It seems like every girl I pick up uses the name Smith. Now you either give me your real name, or I'll think up a better one than that!"

This truck driver had too many answers. Apparently I wasn't the first girl he had picked up along the highway. This was making me nervous. By the time we reached New York City, he would be expecting me to pay him for the trip, and I wasn't about to give him the kind of payment I thought he had in mind!

I tried and tried to think of a name, but my mind was blank.

Finally he said, "Okay, here's a name for you: Lynn Cramer."

"Lynn Cramer? That's not my name."

"Of course I know that's not your name. But my name is John Cramer, and since you're my daughter, you're Lynn Cramer. Now don't forget that."

I didn't like the way he ordered me around. That wasn't what I had in mind in my dreams of freedom. Anyway, maybe when we stopped, I'd find a way to ditch this burly truck driver. He was making me more and more nervous.

When we pulled into the truck stop, the lot was crowded with other semis. Most of the drivers were inside having coffee.

When Mr. Cramer and I walked in, all heads turned our way. A couple of drivers whistled. Then one yelled, "Hey, John, I didn't know you got married again." Then he started to laugh.

John pointed his huge finger at the guy. "Listen,

buddy, this here is my daughter Lynn. One more remark like that out of you, and I'll slap you silly."

Everybody laughed—even John. They all knew I was a runaway and a pickup. Not much chance to ditch John now.

We slid into opposite sides of a booth and ordered coffee and pie. A young, handsome truck driver came over, slid into the booth next to me, and half-whispered, "How much do you charge?"

I wanted to belt him, but Mr. Cramer was laughing. I wasn't in much of a position to be choosy about my associates, so I knew I had to stifle my feelings.

"She's not for sale, Tom," Mr. Cramer said. "Now get lost."

I sat there quietly, but on the inside I really wanted to scratch that young smart aleck's eyes out. I might not have been a good girl all my life, but there was one thing for sure: I was no prostitute. The very idea of it made me feel dirty all over.

I was about halfway through my piece of pie and was absentmindedly staring at the front door, wondering how I could get out of there and away from John and these other truck drivers. Just then the door opened, and in walked two New York State policemen. They stood there looking around the diner, now and then nodding to drivers they knew. Then they spotted me and headed straight our way. Had they already found out about my running away from the Greens?

John Cramer was staring down his coffee cup, half-asleep. "Cramer," I whispered, "the cops!"

He jerked up straight and spun around. By that time the cops were standing beside us.

"Young lady, do you have some identification?" one of them asked.

"I sure do. It's out in my dad's truck. Do you want me to go get it?"

John Cramer spoke up. "It's okay, officer. This is my daughter Lynn. She's not what you think."

"Oh, I'm sorry," the officer replied. "It's just that it seemed rather strange to see a teenager in here with all these truck drivers at this hour of the night. Just for the record, we'll have to see her identification."

"Oh, for crying out loud, officer," John said. "Don't you believe me?"

"Aw, get off it, will you?" the officer said. "You've been around for a while, and I've been around. No father with any sense would bring a good-looking young lady like this into a place full of truck drivers at this hour of the morning."

John bristled. "You're talking about my buddies," he said.

"Just hold on," the officer said as he backed off a little. "If her identification matches yours, there's no problem." Then he motioned to me. "Come on, young lady. Let's walk out to the truck and check your identification."

John was really fired up now. He stood, protesting, "Listen, officer, you'd better know what you're doing, because I'm going to sue you for false arrest!"

The officer smiled. "This is no arrest. This is just asking for identification. Certainly a little thing like that wouldn't upset you, would it? You just told me she's your daughter. So I believe that as soon as I look at her identification, everything's going to be okay. Now sit back down and finish your coffee. I promise that I'll take good care of her."

John slumped back into the booth, and the officer took me by the arm. "Okay, let's go," he said.

Now what was I going to do? It wouldn't take them long to figure out I was a runaway, and John would squeal to save his own hide. He'd tell them exactly where he picked me up.

I turned around to look at him. He didn't even seem concerned about my predicament. In fact, he was over whispering something to one of his buddies.

All the way across that big parking lot, I was wondering what I was going to do. Should I make a run for it? Out of the question. These tall, lanky officers could outrun me anytime.

We got to John's truck, and I reached up for the door handle, pretty much resigned that there was no way out of this situation. I'd be placed in a jail and then back into foster care, or maybe even an institution. That would be the pits!

As I reached for the door handle, I glanced into the rearview mirror and detected someone running toward us. Then I heard him screaming: "Officers! Officers! Come quick! There's been a terrible accident!"

I turned at the same time the officers did. That guy —he looked sort of familiar. Oh, yes. He was the one I saw John Cramer whispering to when we were going out.

The guy yelled excitedly, "There's been a terrible accident on up the highway. I saw two bodies lying on the pavement. We were trying to reach you on our CBs, but we couldn't. Maybe you were inside here. Anyway, you need to radio for an ambulance. It's really a bad one!"

One of the officers looked at me and said, "You're lucky this time, young lady."

With that the two of them ran for their car, flipped

on the siren and lights, and fishtailed out of the lot,
spewing gravel all over the place.

I opened the truck door and grabbed my bag, all the
time keeping an eye on the diner. I could see John
sitting there by the window, watching in the direction
that the police had gone.

And then I saw that other driver hightailing it for his
rig and taking off—in the opposite direction of the
police!

I zigzagged across the parking lot, hiding behind
some trucks when I could. I was trying to stay out of
Cramer's line of vision. Somehow I had to get away
from him. I just knew he would be expecting me to pay
him for the trip. But how was I going to get out of
there?

Besides, I didn't feel any safer with any of the other
truck drivers. They all seemed to have the same thing
on their minds.

I stopped short as a customer came out of the diner.
Another truck driver? No. This one walked over to his
car and got in. Then as soon as he started out of the
driveway, I ran as fast as I could and held up my hands.
He stopped.

I flung open the passenger-side door and panted,
"Please, can you help me? This filthy-minded truck
driver is going to rape me. Please help me."

"Quick! Get in!" the man commanded.

I jumped in and threw my bag into the backseat. He
headed down the highway toward New York. Another
lucky break.

As we drove along, he said, "Okay, tell me what
happened."

"Oh, I just ran into some bad luck," I responded.
"I'm making my way to New York City from Ohio and

got as far as Binghamton. I wanted to save money and decided to hitchhike. This big, burly truck driver picked me up. While we were driving along, he kept rubbing my leg and making all sorts of suggestive remarks. Then he decided to give me a good meal. I ate a big one back there at the diner, but I knew eventually he would be expecting me to pay him off. You know how it is. They feed you good, but then those dirty old men want dessert. Know what I mean?"

He laughed.

"Now I wouldn't say that all truck drivers are that way," he told me. "There are many wonderful men driving these semis. I'm a salesman myself. I've been one for years, and I've done an awful lot of traveling. I've met a lot of truck drivers over the years, and I think the vast majority of them will help out anybody in trouble."

I didn't know if he was buying my story or not. Maybe I should soften it a little.

"Well, maybe it wasn't quite as bad as I imagined," I said. "But I was in a truck, and I didn't know what to do."

"Well, young lady," he said, "let me give you some fatherly advice. Any young girl out hitchhiking at four-thirty in the morning can open herself to a lot of trouble. I mean, a lot of trouble."

"Trouble? What kind of trouble?"

"I think you know what I'm talking about," he said.

My body stiffened. I just didn't like the way he said that. I glanced over at him. It almost seemed as if he were leering at me. What did this guy have on his mind? Now what had I gotten myself into?

3   Rapes occurred frequently, I knew. But was I about to become a victim?

The man drove for some distance without saying anything. Then up ahead I noticed an exit. He seemed to slow a little when he saw the sign. Was he going to turn off and take me to some deserted back road? Dumb me. If only I had stayed with that truck driver, I probably would have had a better chance. People get suspicious of eighteen-wheelers on back roads!

As unobtrusively as possible, I studied the guy. I needed to be able to identify him. Under other circumstances I would have said he was kind of good-looking. His suit was well tailored, and he didn't seem to be the kind of guy who might have rape on his mind. But I knew that rapists came in all sizes and shapes.

Sure enough, we edged off the main highway and onto that exit road. Up ahead I spotted a stop sign. Good! As soon as he came to a stop there, I would fling open the door and take off. He wouldn't dare try anything with all the other traffic along the highway.

As we slowed for the stop sign, my fingers tightened around the door handle. Every muscle in my body tensed in anticipation of what I was going to do.

But as we neared the stop sign, I noticed that he wasn't slowing. Instead he quickly looked one way and then the other and wheeled around the corner without stopping. We were going too fast for me to try to jump.

Then he said, "Do you mind if we stop a minute?"

His voice startled me. "Huh?" I responded.

"I just asked if you mind if we stop for a minute."

I glared at him. I couldn't be sure whether or not this was a proposition. But what could I say? "Yeah, I guess it's okay."

To the right I noticed a gas station. He pulled up and stopped by the men's room. He mumbled something about having had too much coffee and was gone.

As soon as he stepped out of the car, I breathed easier. At least it was no rape—yet. For a fleeting moment I thought of taking off with his car. If anybody caught me, I could always say I was fleeing from a rapist. I looked at the steering column. No luck. He had taken the keys with him. No car stealing for me!

I sat there trying to figure out my next move. Should I jump out and run for it now? Or was this guy okay? Maybe the next guy really would be a rapist. I'd better wait it out. I had to get to New York City somehow.

I must have been lost in thought because suddenly someone knocked on my window right next to my ear. I jumped so high I almost hit the roof! Then I heard a raucous laugh, and I turned to find the source.

Peering into my window was one of the grubbiest men I had ever seen.

"Hey, girl," he said, "didn't mean to scare you to death. You okay?"

"Yeah, I'm okay now, but you really did frighten me."

It's hard to tell the age of a bum like that. I guess maybe he was about thirty. Stubble covered his face. His clothes were tattered and dirty.

"Hey, girl, you wouldn't happen to be heading down the road to New York City, would you?"

I started to say yes, but I caught myself. This guy looked like a bum. Besides, I had no right to invite him to ride in someone else's car. Neither could I tell him I was a runaway.

"You going to New York?" he repeated.

How was I going to answer him? If I said no, the driver would soon come out of the men's room and he might decide to give the bum a ride. Then because I lied, the bum might know that something suspicious was up.

I didn't have to answer, for at that moment the driver came out and headed for his car. The bum spotted him and started toward him. I couldn't hear the conversation, but I could see the driver shaking his head no.

As they got closer to the car, the bum started to yell. He was gesturing wildly, trying to make his point. Finally they got to the car, and the driver opened the door. I heard him say, "No sir, I'm very sorry, but I just can't take you with us. I mean, you know how it is."

"Why you dirty good-for-nothin' so-and-so!" the bum countered. "Can't you help out a guy who is desperate? My wife and five kids are waiting for me in New York City, and I don't have a dime to my name to get there."

The driver wasn't buying that story, and neither was I. The bum obviously was a con artist who would say anything to get his way—a ride or money.

As the driver tried to get into the car, the bum grabbed him and spun him around. Then the bum cocked his arm and started to throw his fist.

What happened next was so fast I really couldn't believe it. I saw that bum go sailing through the air and land on his back!

I jumped out of the car to see if I could help. But

almost before I got the car door open, the bum had jumped to his feet. In his right hand a switchblade flashed. Open!

With a scream he lunged at the driver. But the driver grabbed his arm, turned around, flipped him over, and the bum went sailing through the air the second time. He hit the ground with a tremendous *whomp!*

I glanced back at the driver. He stood there with his feet apart, and he even had the bum's switchblade in his hand. I didn't know how in the world he could have done that.

"Okay, buddy, you want to try again?" the driver yelled.

The bum slowly got to his feet. I tensed. Would he go after the driver again? He would! But this time the driver did a karate chop. The bum lay out cold on the parking lot.

The driver muttered, half to himself, "Real stupid, buddy; real stupid. If you only knew who you were trying to attack!"

Those words shocked me almost as much as the way the driver had been able to take care of himself. Who was this man, anyway? I'd never seen anyone defend himself as well as he had.

He turned to me. "Here, give me a hand. We'll drag him over and prop him against the wall. He's not traveling anywhere for a little while."

The driver grabbed the bum by his shoulders. I picked up his feet, and we half carried, half dragged him over to the building and propped him up against the wall. He looked absolutely stupid there.

"I think it'll be a little while before he tries something like that again," the driver said, dusting off his trousers.

Then he did something that flabbergasted me. He folded up the switchblade and handed it to me!

"Here, take this," he said. "You're going to need it where you're going."

I turned the thing over in my hand several times. It looked so mean and awesome.

"Thanks, mister, but I don't know how to handle one of these. I mean, what would I ever do with a switchblade?"

"You said you were going to New York City, didn't you? Well, let me tell you, kid, you're going to need it there. Here, let me give you a lesson."

Who was the man, anyway? He knew karate. He knew how to defend himself, even against a switchblade. Now he was going to give me a lesson on how to use a switchblade. I guess I must have read him wrong earlier. A man with rape on his mind isn't likely to give his intended victim a switchblade and teach her how to use it! He took the switchblade out of my still-open hand and dropped the knife inside his shirt.

"Okay, supposing some guy comes at you, here's what you do."

He deftly reached inside his shirt. As he pulled out the switchblade, he flicked it open with the same motion. Then he stuck the switchblade straight out and yelled, "Stop or I'll kill you!" His eyes were full of anger.

I jumped back, terrified. "No! No!" I screamed.

Then he laughed. "Okay, kid, now listen to this. It'll help you."

I couldn't believe what was happening. Here in a parking lot on the way to New York City in the wee hours of the morning, some stranger was demonstrating how I was supposed to defend myself! What did he really know about me? Or suspect?

"As you pull the switchblade out," he went on, "you flick it open on the movement outward. Then you scream and look as mean as you can and really feel in your heart that you're going to kill this guy. What you've got to remember is this: *Fear affects everybody!* As soon as a person is afraid of you, he'll back off. So with the switchblade pointed straight at him and you screaming that you're going to kill him—that will at least momentarily stop the worst murderer in the country!"

He handed the switchblade back and instructed, "Okay, now, put it in your bra, and let's practice."

I started to do as he said, but I was so embarrassed with him watching me.

"Go ahead. The first time it will feel funny, but you'll get used to it."

He was absolutely right. It did feel bulky and cold.

I dropped my hands to my sides. Then he lunged at me, screaming, "I'm going to kill you!"

I turned and started to run, but he grabbed me by the shoulders. "No! No! No! We're just practicing! Don't you remember?"

My heart was beating like crazy. I was nervous about running away, and I couldn't figure out what this guy was up to.

"Okay," he said, "let's try it again. I'm going to lunge toward you. When I do, you reach in and grab that switchblade."

This time I determined to get it right. He lunged. I reached into my bra, but as I started to pull the switchblade out, my hand got tangled in the strap. By this time he had his arms around me.

"I see you'll need quite a bit of practice," he said patiently. "Here, try it a few times with me just standing here."

I reached into my bra, and this time I got my hand on the switchblade. I jerked it out. Then with the other hand, I pushed the button to open it. Nothing happened. I pushed it some more. Still nothing. I bent over to see what I was doing wrong, and suddenly the blade snapped out, almost cutting off my nose!

"Goodness, you're uncoordinated," he said. "You look as though you were raised on a farm or something."

I chuckled. "Well, kind of. I've been raised all over the place."

"Oh, is that right?"

Now he was getting too personal. I didn't want to tell him anything else about my past.

"Listen, kid," he announced, "I think you and I have played games long enough. I know you're a runaway. The only reason I picked you up was that I knew you could trust me. You might have gotten yourself into a whole lot of trouble with the next guy coming along. I'm a family man and have no thoughts in mind to hurt you in any way. I've got a job I'm proud of, and I help a lot of people. So, since I got that off my chest, why don't you tell me your name?"

"Hey, mister, no way. I mean, no way."

"Okay, then, have it your way. I'm going to call you Willamena Stezenheimer."

"Willamena Stezenheimer? That's not my name."

"Of course it isn't. But since you won't tell me what your name is, that's what I'm going to call you."

That would never do. So what if he knew my name? "Okay," I blurted out, "my name is Debbie Carter."

"That's better. Now do you want to know my name?"

"Yeah."

"Adolf Hitler."

I laughed. "Now come on. I told you my real name."

"Okay," he responded. "I'm Ralph Jackson."

"Jackson, huh? That's a pretty common name. I think you made that one up too."

"Well, I think you just made up the name Debbie Carter."

"No way! I didn't make up that name! That's my real name."

"Well, Ralph Jackson is my real name too. You call me Ralph, and I'll call you Debbie. Okay?"

"Okay, Mr. Jackson—er, Ralph. But I don't know if I can believe you. Furthermore, I don't know if I can trust you." Then I told him how I had almost jumped out of his car when he had exited from the highway to stop here.

"Well, Debbie, if I were you, I wouldn't trust me either," he told me. "You never know."

Now why would he say that? Here I was finally starting to feel safe with the guy, and then he throws that out at me. Was he merely trying to get on the good side of me and later on proposition me? Well, I was going to have to take my chances. At least I now had a switchblade—although I knew I wouldn't be any match against him with it.

"All right, let's practice a couple more times with that switchblade, Debbie."

I kept working and working at it and finally started getting it right.

"Hey, Debbie, you're doing better. Now don't forget that that switchblade can come in mighty handy. Sometimes people are a lot more afraid of getting cut than getting shot. So don't forget that element of fear. I mean, really put the fear in them. If you have to tell a couple of lies, tell them you've chopped up other people and aren't afraid to slash them to pieces. Get real mean!"

Lies? That had never been a problem for me!

I slipped the switchblade back into my bra.

"Ralph, can you wait a minute? I guess I'd better go to the bathroom. This has been almost too much for me."

I walked over to the ladies' room and shut the door. Then I heard a car door slam and tires squeal. Don't tell me that was Ralph taking off?

I quickly opened the door. No car! He *had* taken off. But why? He seemed so genuinely to want to help me.

I let out a stream of cuss words. Then I looked over at the gas pump. There was a New York State Police car.

I quickly shut the door. Had I gotten it closed in time? Had they seen me or heard me? Maybe they even saw that bum we had dragged over alongside of the building and would be coming around to investigate.

I knew I had nothing else to do but stay where I was until they were gone. Maybe they were the same two who had questioned me at that truck stop. Or maybe those two had radioed in a report, and all the other state police were looking for me now. Here I was away from the Greens for just a few hours, and already I had gotten into some serious scrapes with the law!

After a few minutes I heard a car drive away. I

waited a little longer, then I eased the rest room door open slightly. I couldn't see any police car. So I edged my way out along the building, hiding behind some bushes until I could be sure the coast was clear. The police were nowhere in sight.

By this time the eastern sky was beginning to streak with the light of a new day. What would it bring for me?

For one thing, I was dead tired. I hadn't slept all night. Maybe I should lie down and rest awhile. But that might not be safe either. I suspected it would be a lot easier for a runaway to get lost in the crowds of New York City than it would be along a highway!

I headed back to the highway and stuck out my thumb as an eighteen-wheeler barreled down on me. He honked, but he didn't even slow down.

I put out my thumb as another car approached. He didn't even honk. Don't tell me it was going to be hard to get a ride in the daylight. The ones with Cramer and Ralph had come so easily, but maybe the new day was bringing me some bad luck.

I kept sticking out my thumb, and cars kept whizzing on by. So I started walking.

As another car approached, I stuck out my thumb again. Good! This one was slowing down. A man was driving, and a woman was seated beside him. I'd be safe with them. He stopped quite a way down the highway, and I ran to where he was.

As I opened the door on the passenger's side, the woman screamed, "Don't get in! Don't get in!"

"What's the matter, lady?" I asked, puzzled. "Is something wrong?"

"No, it's you!" she said. "Don't get in!"

"Okay, lady, have it your way!" I said as I slammed the door.

They took off, spraying gravel all over me. Two pebbles hit my face. Wow! Did they ever sting! Almost instinctively I reached for my new switchblade. That woman was going to be my first victim. But, of course, she was already far down the road.

I kept wondering what was with her. I didn't look that mean, did I? I glanced at my jeans and sweat shirt. I guess I did look pretty scruffy. And with all the stories surfacing these days about hippies and all, maybe . . . .

I didn't have too long to ponder the situation because I saw another car coming. I tried to brush myself off as best I could, and then I stuck out my thumb again. Great! This one was slowing before he ever got to me. I wondered what kind of a character this ride was going to be with.

The car stopped just in front of me. When I ran toward it, was I in for a surprise! "Ralph Jackson!" I exclaimed. "For crying out loud, what are you doing here?"

He chuckled. "Now I don't know if you're going to believe me, Debbie, but when you went into that rest room, a state police car pulled in for gas. He looked my way, and I thought, *The only thing I need right now is for Debbie to walk out of that rest room and get into my car!* Those state cops can spot a runaway anywhere. If he came over and learned you were a runaway, well, it would have been all over for both of us."

Uh huh! Ralph must be into the rackets and is fleeing from the law. But what kind of racket? A bank robber? Or what was there about him that he didn't want an encounter with the police?

"Get in, Debbie," he ordered. "Quick! Before that cop comes by again!"

He didn't have to tell me twice. Although I really didn't know what kind of a guy he was, I did feel somewhat safe with him. And he did seem concerned about what happened to me.

As we drove toward the city, we both sat in silence. I was worn out from what I had been through, but I still couldn't sleep. For one thing, I wasn't sure I could trust him. For another, my curiosity got the best of me. So I thought I might as well ask him what he was up to.

"What kind of work do you do?" I asked gingerly. "You said you were a salesman?"

"Kind of."

"What do you mean, kind of? What do you sell?"

"I guess you could say I sell services."

"What kind of services?"

"Now, Debbie, I really can't tell you anything beyond that. I've told you my name, and it's my real name. I told you I sell services, but that's as far as I can go. Okay?"

Who was this guy? Something sure was different about him. And why was he so skittish around the police?

I tried a couple of indirect approaches and got the same kind of rebuff. So we sat there silently, and finally I dozed a little. When I opened my eyes, we were crossing the George Washington Bridge and heading toward Manhattan.

"How far you going?" I asked.

"Well, Debbie, let me put it this way. How far are *you* going?"

"Oh, I really don't know, Ralph. I got nowhere special to go. I guess you can just let me out anywhere."

"Listen, Debbie, New York City is one of the worst places in the world to run away to. As soon as you hit those streets, the pimps will be after you."

"Yeah, I know all about that," I answered. "I grew up in Brooklyn."

"Debbie, I know that no matter what I say, I can't change your mind about staying here in the city. But you'll end up on the streets like a lot of other runaways. You'll be broke—nowhere to go, nothing to eat. Then they're going to get you, and you're going to be out there prostituting. And then, so you can cover up how you're losing your self-respect, you'll become a drug addict."

"Mr. Jackson, Ralph, I mean, you have me all wrong. You're talking to Debbie Carter. I'll get a job and earn a lot of money and make a name for myself. And I'm not about to get full of venereal diseases like those filthy prostitutes. I'm just a girl who has had a few tough breaks in life, but I'm going to change all that! I know what I'm doing!"

I wished I felt as sure as I sounded.

"Debbie, Debbie, I've heard that same story a thousand times."

I studied him. Who in the world was this guy?

"Now listen, Debbie," he went on. "Here's what I'm going to do. I'm going to drop you off at the YWCA. Do you have any money?"

"No, I really don't."

"Okay, I'm going to give you twenty dollars. You are to take that money and use it to stay overnight at the Y. After you get some sleep, ask the lady at the desk to tell you where you can stay. They have places for runaways here. They'll give you the names of a couple of fine organizations that help runaways. You go to one of them. Now don't be afraid to do that. And don't give false information. These people won't pressure you or turn you over to the police. There are people here in the city who do these things for people like you. The big problem is that a lot of runaways don't know about this, and I want you going in the right direction. Do you understand what I'm saying?"

"Ralph, why are you being so nice to me?" I asked. Then I bowed my head. All the tension and uncertainty overwhelmed me, and I couldn't stifle the tears.

He reached over and began to pat me on the shoulder. "Now, now, Debbie, you just act real tough. If you do what I say, I think you're going to make it. You have great potential."

I couldn't shut off the tears, but soon we pulled up in front of a large building. I noticed the YWCA sign.

Ralph pulled out his billfold. He sure had the money! He thumbed through the bills and handed me a twenty. "Here, Debbie."

I looked at him, and then I looked at the twenty. Somehow I just couldn't take charity. "Could you give me your address, Ralph? As soon as I get a job, I'll pay you back."

He smiled. "No, I just couldn't do that, Debbie. I've told you all I can about me. Besides, this is something that I really want to do to help you."

Now he had tears in his eyes too.

"Debbie," he went on, "I know you're wondering why I'm doing this. Well, I'll tell you this much. I have three beautiful daughters at home and a wonderful wife. This may shock you, but I worked for the New York City Police Department for fifteen years as a detective. I became pretty well known and decided to go into business for myself. I'm a private detective."

So that was it. That was why he was able to disarm that bum so quickly. But why was he afraid of the police?

"Okay, Ralph, but how come you were so afraid of the police?"

He chuckled. "Listen, if those state patrolmen had asked for my identification and your identification, can you imagine how it would appear for a private detective to be breaking the law by picking up a hitchhiker? That's why I had to take off."

So that was it.

"And, Debbie, please do what I tell you, and you'll survive this jungle. But otherwise you won't."

I leaned over and kissed him on the cheek.

"I believe God has a beautiful plan for your life, Debbie. Don't mess it up."

I drew back in surprise at that comment. "You really think God is interested in someone like me?" I asked.

"Well, Debbie, I may not be as good a Christian as I should be, but I believe God has a beautiful plan for everybody's life. The great problem He has is that He can't convince people to follow Him. If you really follow the Lord, Debbie, it will be so different for you. God really wants to take care of you."

I didn't reply. I simply got out of the car, grabbed my duffel bag, and mumbled a word of thanks. It was too emotional a moment to say more.

I slammed the car door and turned toward the YWCA; and Ralph Jackson was gone.

Did God really care about me? Was He really concerned about my future, like that judge had told me several years ago? And how could I find out?

Well, here I was in New York City anyway, and with

my honor still intact. Would I have to become a prostitute to support myself? Would I end up as a junkie like most runaways? Or would I be the one who was able to be different?

4

The YWCA building looked old and not very inviting. But at least it was a place to stay. I walked up the steps slowly, pushed open the door, and walked across the lobby to a counter where a woman was standing. She watched my every move, but I really didn't care. I was so tired that all I wanted was to take a shower and get some sleep.

How much would a room cost? I knew New York City was expensive, and I was hoping that it wouldn't be any more than twenty dollars. But if it was that much, where was I going to get money to eat? Well, I could figure that out later.

"How much is a room?" I asked as cheerfully as I could.

"How long are you going to stay?"

"Oh, just one night. I'm in town for just today and tonight, and then I'm moving on."

"I'm sorry, honey, but we only have rooms available for people who are planning to stay at least a week."

"A week? But I wanted to stay just one night. I can't stay a week."

"Listen, girl, you look tired. Let me make a deal with you. Why don't you just give me the money for a week's stay. Then tomorrow, when you check out, I'll give you a refund. You see, the big shots around here told me to rent for a minimum of a week, but they have

soft spots in their hearts and will give people their
money back if they have to check out. And let me tell
you something else. It's a lot safer here than in some
of those dungeons around town. I mean, it's real bad
out there, girl."

I knew that twenty dollars wasn't going to get me
through a week. What was I going to do now?

"Is it a deal?" she asked as she interrupted my
thoughts.

"Well, how much do you charge by the week?"

"Just seventy-two dollars and fifty cents. That isn't
much. Of course, the room is small, but it's clean. And
you'll have to use the bathroom down the hall. But let
me tell you, girl, if you were staying at the Hilton,
you'd have to pay more than that for one night! Not
a bad price, hey?"

"Yeah, I guess that's a good price, but since I'm
only going to stay one night, I don't think I'll do it that
way."

"Let me tell you something, girl. I know this is your
first day in New York City. You've probably heard that
everybody rips you off here. But not the YWCA. Like
I say, give me seventy-two dollars and fifty cents. Then
tomorrow when you check out, I'll give you a refund.
But you'll have to keep your mouth shut about it.
Okay?"

I just couldn't bring myself to tell her that I had only
twenty dollars. If she knew I was a runaway, she'd
probably call the cops. Somehow I had to bluff my way
out of this. So I said, "Isn't that arrangement dishonest?"

She bristled. "Listen, girl, I'm trying to give you a
break. Don't try to give me no sermon!"

"I'm not giving you any sermon!" I shot back. "I

just asked you a question. Don't you think what you're proposing is dishonest?"

"Listen, you snotty little brat, you get out of here before I call the cops. A runaway like you should be behind bars! Now get out!"

"Hold it! Hold it!" I retorted. "Don't yell at me like that. Just keep your big lip shut!"

"Get out of here before I call the cops!" she yelled again. "Do you hear me?"

I stood there gritting my teeth, trying to keep cool. "Listen, you big, fat slob," I countered, "if you're what the YWCA is all about, I think I've made a big mistake. I thought this was supposed to be a good, helpful organization." Then with all the sarcasm I could muster, I spit it out: "Oh, you're a fine representative! You're the one who ought to have your mouth busted and be thrown out on the street!"

That did it! The woman exploded and reached out to grab me. I jumped back, and before I really knew what I was doing, I had whipped out my switchblade. I pushed the button, and it came open—the first time!

When she saw the blade she backed up. "Okay, girl, okay. Have it your way. So I'm a big, fat slob and shouldn't be representing the YWCA. But listen, just quietly fold up that switchblade and walk on out that door. I mean, you and I can't afford trouble. Understand?"

I pushed the button and bent the blade back into the handle and stuck the knife back into my bra. Then I wheeled around and walked out the door—with a sense of power. One thing was sure. That switchblade made me a big woman. And I had a sneaking suspicion that someday it was going to save my life.

Now where? I started walking. New York City is such

a strange place. So many different types of people.
And so much dirt! But the more I walked, the cleaner
it got. I finally came to a park. This must be the famous
Central Park.

Water gushed from a large fountain, and I walked
over and sat on the edge of it to rest. It was such a
serene setting—so opposite to the turmoil I had been
through.

I sat there daydreaming. Somehow I had to figure
out a place to stay. Then I remembered what Ralph
had told me about the agencies here in the city that
took care of runaways. Should I go to one of them? At
least it would be a place to stay and something to eat.
But would they turn me in and would I have to go back
to wherever the social workers wanted me to go? No,
I'd come this far on my own. I wasn't going to give in
yet.

I was sitting there staring at the ground when I
heard footsteps, and a man stopped right in front of
me. I could tell that his shoes looked expensive. My
eyes slowly moved up his body until I was looking into
the eyes of one gorgeous hunk of a man smiling
widely.

"Hey, good-looking, what's up?" he asked.

All I could manage was a weak smile. "Aw, nothing
much," I told him. "I was just sitting here enjoying
this gorgeous fountain."

"Looking at fountains?" he answered. "Hey, baby,
you don't look like a tourist to me. You look like a girl
who's out for a good time. And, baby, I can give you
a good time!"

This guy was handsome, expensively dressed, and
looking for a girl. I must look like a bum. Why would
he . . . ? Oh, oh! He must be a pimp!

I had to get out of there. So I stood up and started to walk away. He followed. "Hey, baby, don't turn me off that way. Where are you going?"

If I only knew!

I kept walking. When I felt his hands on my shoulders, I quickly wheeled around and pushed them off. "Get your hands off me, you creep!" I ordered.

He fell back in feigned horror. "Hey, you're a spunky little one, aren't you? You mad at your old man and old lady?"

"It's none of your business who I'm mad at. You just mind your own business and pick on another girl. I'm not about to get associated with some creepy pimp!"

"Hey, wait a minute!" he responded. "I may be creepy, but I'll tell you one thing, baby. I'm not a pimp. And that's the truth."

I stopped and looked him over. Had I made a mistake in my judgment? Or would a pimp ever admit to being a pimp?

"Listen," I said, "I know how you guys operate. My sister ran away from home once and came here. She got hooked up with a pimp, and he made a slave out of her. You guys are all the same. Real slick, dress nice, and full of lies."

"So why are you running away?" he asked.

"What do you mean, why am I running away? I'm not running away. My old man and old lady live here in New York City, and I'm just staying cool. That's all."

"Ha!" he laughed sarcastically. "I don't know what I'm going to do with you, baby. You're so full of lies that you stink. Listen, I've been here on the streets for years. I know all about you girls. Now don't josh me any more."

This guy obviously was a smart dude. But I really didn't trust him.

"How about some breakfast?" he asked. "You look starved."

Food! That would solve one of my problems. But if this guy bought my breakfast, would he want something else?

He must have read my thoughts. "Come on now," he said, "trust me. I'll tell you what. I'm going to take you over to this nice little restaurant. The waitresses over there know me. I'll have them tell you what kind of a guy I am. Okay?"

This dude was sure persistent; and I was sure hungry. Since I had nothing else to do, I might as well take a chance. After all, I was too smart to be taken in by some pimp.

"Okay, I'll have breakfast with you," I said, "but if you try anything funny, I'll call the cops."

"Listen, baby, relax, will you? You're not going to have to call any cops. I'm just a plain, ordinary guy who likes to help out a damsel in distress."

"Okay, if you're such a plain, ordinary guy, let's start by your telling me your name and what you do."

"Well, my name is Steve DiSilva. What's yours?"

Should I give him a false one? I was trying to think of one when he interrupted my thoughts. "Now listen, I didn't give you a false name. I gave you my real name, and I want your real name!"

This guy sure was shrewd.

"Okay, I'm Debbie Carter."

"You sure?"

"Oh, for crying out loud. You don't believe a word I say, do you? My name really is Debbie Carter."

"Okay, Debbie, I believe you on that one. But I sure wish you'd quit lying about your past."

"Steve, I will if you will."

He looked hurt. "Hey, man, like I said, I'm telling you the truth. And in just a few minutes you're going to find out about me."

We walked a couple of blocks and into a rather classy coffee shop. He pointed toward a booth.

When we were seated, Steve motioned toward a waitress. "Hey, Myrtle, come over here a minute."

When she got up close, he said, "Myrtle, am I a pimp?"

Wow! He sure was out in the open about it!

Myrtle looked at me and then back at Steve. "Are you a what?" she repeated.

"I said, 'Am I a pimp?' "

She laughed uproariously. "Steve, you would probably make a great astronaut or president of a bank, but I don't know about you and the pimp business. Why, if your life depended on pimping, you'd go broke!" Then she laughed again.

"See, Debbie, what did I tell you?" Steve asked. "Myrtle knows I'm a good boy."

"Well, what do you do?" I asked.

Steve's smile faded quickly. I glanced at Myrtle. When her eyes met mine, she turned and walked away.

What was Steve really into?

Another waitress came over and handed us the menus. But I sat there studying Steve rather than the menu. What was this good-looking hunk of a man up to?

Finally I could contain my curiosity no longer, and I leaned across the table and whispered, "Tell me, Steve, what do you do?"

He looked me square in the eye and answered, "I'm a pimp."

I pushed out of the booth, but he grabbed my arm. "Sit down!" he ordered.

"But, Steve, you told me you weren't a pimp. I thought I could trust you. You're a filthy liar, just like that dirty Myrtle. I'm getting out of here."

He pulled my arm harder. "Aw, come on, Debbie, can't you take a joke? I'm not really a pimp. You can trust me."

I settled back down in the booth. "Steve, I wish you wouldn't kid like that. I'm very nervous and easily upset. Please, no more jokes."

"Listen, Debbie, I haven't known you very long, but I think there's something we need to get straight. Now tell me: Who are you really?"

I stared at the menu. Should I level with him?

"You'll feel a lot better if you start telling the truth," he coaxed.

"Okay, I'll tell you. You guessed it right. I'm a runaway from upstate New York. I got in town early this morning. I have only twenty dollars on me, and I tried to get a room at the YWCA. The woman wanted a week's rent, so I had a big fight with her. It got kind of dirty. I left there and just walked around and met you over at the park. So help me, Steve, that's the truth."

"That's better," he said as he gently patted my arm.

Now that he knew about me, maybe he would tell me about himself. But before I could ask, he had reached into his pocket and pulled out a huge roll of money. "Here, baby," he said, "here's a hundred bucks. It's yours. You don't have to pay it back."

I stared at that wad of money. If he had more hun-

dreds in there like he had given me, he must have had
thousands of dollars. I just couldn't believe it.

"Here, I want you to have it," he said as he pushed
the bill across the table to me.

"Steve, I just can't accept money from a stranger. I
wasn't brought up that way."

"Oh, Debbie, get off it, will you? You obviously
need the money, so humble yourself and take it. It's
yours. No strings attached. And don't get any smart
ideas. I don't plan to take you to my apartment or
anything like that."

I took the money, folded it, and stuck it in the front
pocket of my jeans. I'd never owned a hundred-dollar
bill before!

"All right, now that's settled, what are you going to
have for breakfast?" Steve asked.

I couldn't concentrate on the menu, so he made up
my mind for me. "How about a couple of scrambled
eggs and sausage and orange juice and a cup of coffee?
That will probably hit the spot."

I smiled. "Yeah, that sounds good."

The waitress finally came back and took our order.
Steve made some small talk about New York City while
we waited for our order and was rather quiet while we
ate. I didn't know what to say either, but I sure was
hoping to find out what this guy was up to. Maybe he
was a rich kid who got an inheritance from his parents.
His hands sure didn't look like he had worked on a
farm. For all I knew, maybe he was a bank robber.
Whatever, he was pretty cagey about it.

We finished our breakfast almost in silence, and
Steve paid the check. Out on the street he said, "Well,
Debbie, I guess this is so long. Take good care of
yourself and watch out for the con artists. They are on

every corner looking for a girl like you. Just stay cool, and maybe you'll make it."

He stuck out his hand, and I shook it. Then he turned and started to walk away.

Now what? I felt so lonely. I simply stood there and watched Steve walk away. He cut across the middle of the block, and I saw a guy approach him. They walked together for a short distance, turned the corner, and then were gone from my sight.

That hadn't worked out quite like I expected, but at least I had one hundred twenty dollars now. That would be enough to stay at the Y for a week. But that fat old lady wasn't about to rent me a room after I pulled a knife on her.

I walked back to Central Park. It was about ten and the late springtime sun was making me so drowsy. I sat on a park bench, leaned over, and soon was fast asleep.

I have no idea how long I slept, but the next thing I remember, someone had his hands over my mouth and eyes. A voice half-whispered, "I'm a pimp, and I gotcha!"

I jerked awake, slapped the hands away, and tried to get my bearings of where I was. As I turned toward the source of the voice, I looked up into a familiar face— Steve!

"Debbie, what in the world are you doing sleeping in the middle of Central Park?" Steve asked with concern. "Don't you know that you're easy prey for a mugger? You could have been hurt!"

I rubbed my eyes and stretched. "I guess I was so tired that I just had to sit down. I didn't plan on falling asleep. But you're right. This is probably not the best place in the world to sleep."

"Well, if you're so sleepy, why don't you come over to my apartment? Nobody's going to get you there."

So this was his approach. He was one of those guys who would get you into his apartment and then try to get you into bed. I wasn't about to let that happen.

Steve must have been reading my thoughts again. "Debbie, you can just flush those thoughts out of your head. You can come over and sleep in my apartment, but not in my bed. I've got a soft, comfortable sofa. You can take a nap there. And don't get any funny ideas or read anything into this invitation."

I laughed. "Oh, Steve, I just don't know about you. That was exactly what I was thinking—that you had some ulterior motives."

"Oh, for crying out loud, Debbie. First you thought I was a pimp. Now when I try to be nice to you again, you think I'm trying to get to you. You probably even thought that about the money. But you're wrong. Like I tell you, I'm not that kind of a guy. You can trust me."

"Okay, I'm sorry for misreading your motives, Steve. But tell me one thing. What do you really do? Why do you carry so much money around?"

"I'm a salesman," he said.

"A salesman? Wow! You really must sell a lot to make that much money!"

"I guess you might say that."

"What kind of things do you sell?"

"Debbie, Debbie, you ask too many questions. Let's just say that I sell highly classified materials. It's a big secret, and very few people know about it. So that's all I can tell you."

Maybe Steve was a spy, buying and selling government secrets or something like that. It sure sounded mysterious.

"Come on, Debbie," Steve said as he took my hand. "You can rest in my apartment for now. But like I say, no funny stuff!"

He took me to a very posh section of the city. I noticed the street sign: Central Park West.

A few blocks later we walked into the lobby of a beautiful apartment building. A doorman let us in and greeted Steve.

We took the elevator to the fourteenth floor, where his apartment was located. It was an absolutely beautiful apartment—so beautiful it almost took my breath away.

He motioned me to a chair, and I sank in it almost up to my ears. "I don't know why I'm doing this for you, Debbie," he told me. "I guess I'm a soft touch. You see, I've got a sister about your age and is she ever giving my parents trouble. She keeps running away, and they just can't handle her. I even thought about bringing her over here, but that might not be too good. So let's just say that you're my kid sister. I'll respect you for that. You can say I'm your big brother.

"There's that soft sofa I was telling you about," he said as he pointed to it. "Just take off your shoes and lie down. I'll get a blanket."

I obeyed; but as I did, my eyes took in the expensive paintings on the wall. The carpet felt so plush and luxurious. Everything here spelled m-o-n-e-y!

Steve soon was back with a beautiful baby-blue blanket, trimmed in satin. He tenderly pulled it over me.

"Okay, Sis, go to sleep. I promise that none of those filthy pimps in New York will be able to lay a hand on you now. And I promise you won't even get mugged!"

I looked up and giggled. "You know, Steve, you really are all right."

He squeezed my chin and then tiptoed out of the room. I closed my eyes in the midst of greater luxury than I ever dreamed existed. Not bad for a little farm girl's first day in New York City.

The next thing I remember was hearing the telephone. Steve tiptoed in and picked it up, half whispering into it: "Like I told you before, I don't want you coming here. I'll meet you at Seventy-second and Broadway."

There was a long pause as he listened to what sounded like an excited voice on the other end. I couldn't make out what the other party was saying.

"Now listen, Manuel, I said you can't come here," Steve said with finality. "And I mean, *can't.* The security guard at the door would not let you in. No! No! This is how I do business. I'll come down to see you in a couple of minutes."

He replaced the receiver and looked over at me.

"Oh, I thought you were still asleep," he said.

"I was till the telephone wakened me."

"Sorry about that. A client of mine wants to see me. I'll be back in just a few minutes. Now you go back to sleep, you little old sleeping beauty."

With that he was gone. As the lock on the door clicked behind him, I lay awake, wondering. Steve was more than a salesman. Of that I was certain. But what was he really?

5   I lay there staring at the ceiling, wondering
what Steve was up to. But I was too tired to think about
it long, and soon I was dozing again. I awakened when
I heard Steve unlock the door.

He saw that I was awake, so he walked toward me.
"Here," he said, "I got you a little something."

I sat up straight, rubbed my eyes, and looked at the
bags he carried. There was one word on them—Saks.
I'd heard of Saks Fifth Avenue. It was a store where the
wealthy shopped.

"What . . . ?" I asked.

"Oh, just a little something for you," he interrupted. I don't want to embarrass you or anything, but
you look a little bedraggled. I thought you might need
a change of clothing."

He handed me the packages—four of them. They
were bulging. I sat down on the floor and began to
look inside. From the first bag I pulled out several
pairs of jeans. "Oh, wow!" I exclaimed. "These are
fantastic! I've never had any fancy ones like these."

"They're a famous fashion line—Calvin Klein," he
told me.

In another bag were some blouses. Just gorgeous.
Steve stood there smiling, obviously proud of himself.

I peeked into the third bag and shut it quickly.
"Steve, how in the world could you buy these for me?"

"Aw, come on; don't be embarrassed. Like I told
you, I have a little sister. I've seen things like those
before."

I peeked in the bag again but didn't pull the contents out. Inside were panties and bras.

In the final bag were a beautiful sweater and a pair of sneakers. I noticed the label on the sweater—cashmere. Wow! I'd never had anything that expensive before!

By this time the bags and clothing were strewn all around me. I just couldn't believe that Steve would go out and buy all those clothes for me. And they all looked like they would fit me.

When I looked up into his face, he was all smiles, but my face turned serious. He read what I was thinking —again. "Aw, come on, Debbie; get off it. None of these will cost you anything. Quit being so nervous about sex. Remember, it's what I said before, you're like my sister."

I giggled. "Okay, Steve, okay. I promise I won't have those thoughts any more."

"That's better," he said, adding, "I don't want to be like your mother or anything, but why don't you go take a nice hot shower? I'm sure you'll feel a lot better after cleaning up and changing your clothes."

I stood up and moved over closer to him. "Steve, can I ask you something?"

"Debbie, I know what you're thinking. No, these are not hot items. If you don't believe me, here are the sales slips. "Oh, one more thing. I had a bargaining session on the sale of a certain item, and I came out very well. I just wanted to share my good luck with you."

"Oh, Steve," I said, "you misread my mind that time. I wasn't going to ask about these items being hot. But I feel good about my change of luck, and I just thought, well, I mean, do you really mind if I . . . "

I faltered in the middle of the sentence and then sat down and began to giggle.

"What's so funny?" Steve demanded.

I struggled back to my feet. Then I stepped over in front of him and said, "May I kiss you—like a little sister to a big brother?"

He joined my laughter. "Why, of course! I mean, after all, why not?"

As I threw my arms around him, he puckered. But I detoured and kissed him on the cheek. He quickly put his arms around me and drew me up close. Gently I pushed him away. "Now, wait a minute, young man," I said, "you're my big brother—and don't you forget it."

"Sorry about that!" Steve laughed. "I guess I was letting my emotions get ahead of me."

We both laughed easily. It felt so good, so right, being here with Steve.

"Come, I'll show you where the bathroom is," he said.

I gathered all the packages up and followed him. When he opened the door, I stared in disbelief. I had never seen a bathroom like this before! At the far end was a huge, sunken tub. You had to climb three steps to get into it. Tropical plants were everywhere. The toilet was in a separate room, off in a corner, and the sink was centered in a huge counter. Everything spelled luxury.

"Here, let me get you a towel."

Steve walked to a closet and pulled out a couple of huge pink towels and washcloths. I've never felt a towel so thick and soft. This would be a shower I would never forget.

Steve backed out the door. "Take your time and enjoy yourself," he said, smiling.

When he shut the door, I locked it. No funny business was going to go on in this bathroom!

I don't know how long I was in that shower, but the longer I stayed, the better I felt. I must have looked awfully grimy. And I couldn't wait to get into those fresh clothes. And to think they came from Saks Fifth Avenue!

When I dressed and walked into the living room, Steve was reading a magazine. "Hey, Debbie," he said admiringly, "you look all right. With all that dirt scrubbed off, you're actually beautiful underneath!"

I felt embarrassed at his compliment and countered, "I'll bet you say that to all the girls."

"Only when Farrah Fawcett comes to see me."

"Farrah Fawcett? You mean *the* Farrah Fawcett, the star who is in movies and TV?"

He nodded.

"Wow! You didn't tell me you had friends like that!"

"Well, Debbie, there're a lot of things you don't know about me. Maybe someday I'll tell you more."

He sat there with a smirk on his face, and I knew he must be kidding. "Aw, come on, Steve; you don't know Farrah Fawcett."

"Well, maybe not," he said, grinning. "But you're almost as beautiful as she is."

That sure made me feel good. I guess everyone likes compliments.

I noticed a different smell throughout the apartment now. Then I noticed something was burning in an ashtray next to Steve. "That sweet smell, Steve; is that some kind of exotic cigarette?"

"Don't you know that smell? I'm smoking a joint."

"A joint? I didn't know you smoked marijuana."

"Oh, every now and then I'll have a joint. But I tell you, the big scene is coke."

"Coke? You mean cocaine?"

"Well, baby, I'm not talking about Coca-Cola. I mean, man, I'm talking about the real thing."

"The real thing? You mean you've got both pot and cocaine?"

"Sure do. Want some?"

"Oh, wow! I've only had a couple of joints in my whole life, and I've never had any coke. I mean, only the groovy people take that stuff. Isn't that right?"

"Well, I guess you might call me groovy. Here, I'll give you some. You'll have to snort it."

"Steve, I have no idea . . . "

"I figured that out," he interrupted. "Watch; I'll show you."

I did, and noticed that when the white powder went up his nose, his hands fell to his side, his eyes got a little glassy, and he said, "Oh, wow! Baby, this is absolutely beautiful!"

He sat there smiling. "I mean, that is good stuff!" he exclaimed over and over again.

That made me anxious to try it.

At first I breathed just a little. "Now a little bit more," Steve instructed. "A little deeper breath."

I felt a tingling sensation in my nose, but I can't adequately describe what happened next. It felt as though I were floating on air. All the tenseness flowed out of my body, and I felt I was absolutely filled with goodness. In my mind I went soaring and floating and felt like I didn't have a problem in the world. I didn't care about Mom Green being frantic about me. I didn't care about running away. I didn't care about the social workers or the police who were out looking for me.

I knew a little about cocaine. Some of the kids talked about it in school—yes, even in upstate New York. With cocaine you get a quick rush that doesn't last a long time like heroin does. They said that cocaine was a cleaner drug. At least you didn't have to use a needle.

As I was coming down from my high, I remembered what Ralph Jackson had warned me about. "You'll become a junkie in the city," he said. I hadn't been here a day, and already I was experimenting with drugs. But his other predictions sure hadn't come true. My luck had been unbelievable. I just knew I was different. No way was I going to get hooked. *I* could handle the stuff!

That evening Steve took me to a fancy restaurant in Central Park—Tavern on the Green. He told me a lot of movie stars ate there. Although he dressed in a suit, he said my jeans were fashionable enough. Then he had second thoughts about the sneakers, so on the way he stopped and bought a pair of high-heeled shoes for me. I'd seen those fancy models wearing jeans and high heels in fashion magazines. Now I was sure I looked just like one of them. I know I sure felt sophisticated.

When we got back to the apartment, I began mentally totaling up all I owed Steve. Would he expect his payment now?

We got inside his apartment, and he shut and locked the door.

He turned toward me. "Want to stay overnight?"

Without a moment's hesitation, I said, "Yes."

Then, much to my surprise, he said, "I have an extra bedroom. You can sleep there."

He walked me to it and opened the door. There was a big, beautiful bed—so plush, so elegant.

"Wait a minute! I'll be right back!" he said as he rushed down the hall.

Oh, oh! Here it comes.

In a few moments he came back and pushed a pair of pajamas into my arms. "I don't imagine you brought any," he said. "In fact, my little sister used to love to wear my pajamas."

"Aw, Steve, you don't have to do this for me. I can sleep without them."

"Don't worry. Besides, they're clean!" Then he laughed.

He stood there in the doorway for a moment. "Debbie, can I ask you a question?"

Now what was he up to? But by now I felt I could trust him, so I responded, "Sure. Why not?"

"Is it okay if I give you a kiss? I mean, like a big brother to a little sister?"

Was this all it was going to cost me? Of course a brotherly kiss would mean absolutely nothing. I smiled up into his face and whispered, "Of course."

Steve tenderly gathered me into his arms. His lips were puckered, so I puckered mine too. Then he slowly brought his lips against mine. It felt like heaven standing there so close to Steve, with his arms around me and our lips holding that tender kiss.

After a few moments he drew back. I looked up and grinned. "Hi, brother."

We both laughed. But I think we were both wondering something. Had I fallen in love with Steve? Had he fallen in love with me?

"Have a good sleep, Debbie," Steve said as he backed out the door. "If the phone rings and I should have to leave, don't worry. Sometimes my work takes me out at odd hours. I've told the security guard at the door that you're my sister. He just laughed at me, and I felt like belting him. But I guess you can't fool those guards."

Steve closed the door behind him as he slipped out. I put on his pajamas. They were way too big, but I still slept in them. This would probably be the closest I was ever going to get to him.

I don't know when I've ever had such a good night's sleep. When I awakened, the sun was shining brightly. I dressed and went out into the living room. No Steve. I looked in the kitchen. No Steve.

Should I knock on his bedroom door? If he was inside, he might misinterpret that. He was probably tired. Maybe he had to go out on business last night when I was sleeping. I decided I'd better not waken him.

But I was famished. I opened the refrigerator. It was stocked with every delicacy one could think of: eggs, bacon, ham, cold cuts, all kinds of fruits and vegetables, beer, champagne.

I pulled out an egg and some ham to fix. I figured Steve wouldn't care. He had enough here to feed an army. I started the egg and put on a pot of coffee.

About halfway through my breakfast, I heard the lock on the front door click. "I hope you didn't mind my fixing some breakfast," I called. "I was starved."

When I didn't get an answer, I headed for the hall. There stood Steve, weaving like a drunken man. His shirt was torn. Blood ran from the corners of his mouth and from his cheek.

"Steve!" I screamed. "What happened?"

"Aw, nothing. Just a little scrape."

"Scrape my foot!" I retorted. You're hurt, and you're hurt bad!"

His shoulder seemed to be injured, and as I reached to examine it, his knees buckled, and he slumped to the floor. I bent over his prostrate form and screamed, "Steve! Steve! Are you all right? Speak to me, Steve!"

I tried to feel his pulse. Nothing. Was he dead? Then I put my ear on his chest. I could still hear a faint heartbeat. I had to get this man to the hospital immediately. I must call an ambulance.

Instinctively I ran to the telephone and dialed the operator. As soon as she answered, I yelled, "I need an ambulance right away." She asked for my address. I didn't know.

Now what?

I asked her to hang on for a minute, and I rummaged through the desk drawer. If I could find a letter addressed to Steve—It worked. There was the address: 5906 Central Park West, Apartment 1402.

I picked up the receiver and repeated the address to the operator. Then she said, "One moment, please."

I waited frantically. Nothing was happening, and every minute counted if we were going to save Steve's life.

Then a voice answered, "City ambulance."

I quickly told him I needed an ambulance and what had happened to Steve. He also asked for the address, and this time, of course, I could tell him right off. Then I shrieked, "Come quick! Steve is almost dead!"

"An ambulance is already on the way, lady. We'll be right there."

I had enough presence of mind to call the doorman

—just in case he thought it was some kind of a trick to get into the building and delayed the ambulance attendants. He had seen Steve come in and didn't seem too surprised.

Then I ran back down the hall to where Steve was still sprawled, unconscious. I had to do something to help him. I ran to the bathroom, got a washcloth, and started wiping his face. Blood was all over it. Then I discovered blood oozing from his side. It looked like he had been stabbed repeatedly.

I ran back for more washcloths, pressing them against the bleeding wounds. If that ambulance didn't get here soon, Steve wasn't going to make it. Then what was I going to do?

Then I heard the siren getting closer and closer. I ran to the window and looked down. Sure enough, there was an ambulance stopped right in front. Two men with a stretcher were heading toward the front door.

I propped the apartment door open and ran to the elevator. By the time I got there, the two men were wheeling the stretcher into the hallway.

"This way!" I called.

They followed me to the apartment. As soon as they saw Steve, they started pulling different things out of their bag. One of them put an oxygen mask over Steve's face; the other began dressing the wounds.

I bent over and asked, "How bad is he?"

"Real bad, ma'am; real bad!"

They quickly lifted Steve onto the stretcher and started toward the door. But as they did that, his eyes fluttered open.

"Debbie? Where am I? Where am I?"

"You're in your apartment, Steve," I answered. "Everything is going to be okay. Don't talk now."

Steve suddenly became aware of the ambulance attendants moving him down the hall. He screamed, "You guys put me down! Right now! Put me down! Right now!"

They ignored his orders. I bent over Steve as we moved down the hall. "Steve, please be quiet. Don't exert yourself. Everything is going to be okay."

That's when he started to curse. "Debbie, for crying out loud, get these guys to stop. I'm all right. I'm all right."

"Steve, you almost died. We've got to rush you to the hospital."

When I said *hospital*, Steve screamed again, "Debbie, do what I tell you! Get back to the apartment! I'll take care of myself."

Then he cussed again. "Please, Debbie, do what I tell you. I mean, whatever you want, I'll give it to you. Just make these guys take me back to the apartment. Everything's going to be all right."

The attendants had finally stopped and were looking to me for direction. Then I thought about the door I had propped open.

"If you're going with us, ma'am, I'd sure lock that door," one of the attendants said. "We'll wait."

I ran back and locked the apartment and hurried back to the elevator just as they were loading Steve in. "Debbie, please don't come with me. Stay in the apartment. And whatever you do, don't let anybody in! Please, Debbie, do what I tell you!"

The exertion was too much for him, and he fell unconscious again. As we were descending on the elevator, one of the attendants said, "Why did he want you to go back to the apartment and stay there? That seems awfully strange."

Yes, it was strange. What was so important about the apartment that Steve wanted me to stay there?

I didn't know the answer to that, but I figured Steve was probably out of his mind with pain and didn't know what he was saying. Maybe his paintings were really valuable, or something. Anyway, I knew it would be best if I went to the hospital with him.

At the hospital they rushed Steve into emergency. The doors closed behind him, and once again I was all alone, with nothing to do but wait and worry.

I paced the hallways for what seemed like an eternity until finally a doctor emerged from behind the closed door.

"Are you related to the young man we just took in there?" he asked me.

What could I say? I'd better lie. "Yes, I'm his sister."

He studied me for a moment and then said, "Well, why don't you sit down and relax. He's going to make it okay."

"Is he conscious yet?"

"Yes, he's just coming out of it. If you want to, you can go in there, but only for a minute. He's still critical."

I followed the doctor to where Steve was lying. But when Steve saw me, he screamed, "Debbie, get out of here! I told you to stay at the apartment! If you're not going to do that, then forget this whole thing."

The doctor said in amazement, "Hey, what's with you two? You certainly don't sound like a loving brother and sister!"

"Keep out of my business," Steve ordered, "but see

if you can't convince Debbie to go back to my apartment and wait there. Tell her, Doc, please."

"Steve," I said, "I meant no problem. Of course I'll go back to the apartment and wait. I meant no problem. I'll go now."

"That's better!" Steve replied, and he seemed to relax. "You go there and wait for me. I'll be out of here in no time."

"How will I get in?"

"Tell the doorman you lost your key. He'll let you in."

As I turned to leave, Steve called, "Debbie, please don't leave that apartment. Don't come to visit me. Just stay there until I get out. We can talk on the telephone, but you must stay there. I mean, you stay *right there!* Don't leave for any reason. I'll tell you later what this is all about. But stay there! Do you promise me?"

That was the strangest request I had ever heard.

"Promise me, Debbie?" Steve demanded again. "I mean, I've got to have your promise!"

"Steve, you don't need my promise. I'll do anything you want me to do. I don't have the greatest memory in the world, but I haven't forgotten where I was two days ago!"

I walked back to his bed and kissed him on the forehead. He just melted and said, "Debbie, I love you. And I love you even more for going back to that apartment. You'll never know how much I love you for doing what I tell you."

The doctor stood there scratching his head. He couldn't figure out what was going on—and neither could I!

All the way back in a cab, I kept wondering what in

the world was in that apartment that I had to be there to guard it. Was I supposed to be guarding some great treasure? Was Steve into some kind of international intrigue? What was it that was so important to him? And why was he so insistent that I stay there?

There had to be something extremely valuable in that beautiful apartment!

6 After such a definite warning, you can believe I stayed put in Steve's apartment. He called from the hospital four times that first day, asking if anyone had come. Then he sternly reminded me I was not to let anyone in, under any circumstances.

By this time I was positive there was something extremely valuable there. But what? And where?

Curiosity got the best of me again, and since I didn't have anything else to do, I began my search. But I was very careful not to leave any evidence that I had been looking. I always replaced things just exactly as he had had them. I pounded on the walls, looked behind pictures for hidden safes, even under all the mattresses. Not a thing.

On the third day when he called again, I had almost decided to ask him why it was so important for me to stay there. But I didn't want to make his recovery any more difficult than it was, so I chickened out.

By the fourth morning I made up my mind that I had to know what was going on. When he called at nine, we exchanged the usual greetings, and he told me he was really beginning to feel like his old self again. That's when I said, "Steve, level with me. Why is it so important that I stay here at your apartment and not leave for anything?"

I waited. And waited. And waited.

"Steve, are you still there?"

"Yeah, I'm here. I was just trying to think of how to answer you."

"Come on, Steve. This is no time for games. Be honest now."

"Will you shut up, Debbie? I don't know how to say this. Besides, my telephone lines might be tapped. If you don't mind, I think it would be best if we waited until I could talk to you privately."

"You mean it's that important?"

"It's extremely important."

"How important?"

"Listen, Debbie, cool it, will you? You saw how battered up I was when I staggered into the apartment. I mean, baby, those knife wounds were from two guys who were out to kill me. Only a miracle saved me."

I had wondered about that often. Why did Steve get stabbed? And who did it?

"Steve, you never have told me about the stabbing. And how come you never did say anything about calling the police?"

"Well, the police have been here at the hospital, Debbie. I didn't tell them anything, and I can't tell you anything now. So quit nagging me. Just stay cool. Keep your eyes open and your mouth shut. Goodbye!" With that he hung up before I could utter another word.

I went to the refrigerator to see what to fix for my breakfast and noticed that the stocks were getting lower. How much longer could I wait in this apartment? I had just started to fix some fruit when the phone rang. Probably it was Steve calling back to apologize for hanging up on me like that. But when I answered, a voice I had never heard demanded, "Who's this?"

I waited. Why did he ask that? Then I blurted out, "None of your business!" and slammed the receiver down.

I knew the telephone would ring again, so I stood there waiting. Sure enough, it did. When I picked it up, a man's voice yelled, "Kid, you listen! You try that one more time, and that will be the end of you! Like we almost did in Steve DiSilva. And if you don't start cooperating, you're going to end up the same way—only worse. We're going to cut your body up into little pieces and throw it into the Hudson River for fish food. Now you hang onto that receiver and listen!"

My body tensed. Then I pulled the receiver from my face and slammed it down again. What in the world was going on around here? I'd better call Steve right away.

I searched the telephone directory for the number at the hospital. But before I could dial it, the phone rang again. I jumped three feet in the air. Was it Steve? Or was it that man? What was I going to do?

The phone rang persistently. If it was Steve and I didn't answer, he would think I had left the apartment, and he'd come flying out of that hospital ready to kill me. But if it was the other guy—well, obviously I didn't want to talk to him.

The phone rang and rang and rang. I had to do something. I slowly picked up the receiver and said, "Hello." A volley of cuss words turned the air blue. I quickly slammed the receiver down again. As soon as I got him cut off, I lifted the receiver off the hook to be sure that nobody called back before I called Steve.

I had lost my place in the phone book, so I went through the whole procedure again. This time when I found the number, I was able to dial it. In just a few moments I heard Steve's voice.

"Steve, what in the world is going on around here? I just received a very threatening phone call. A guy said he was going to stab me to death if I didn't cooperate. I'm scared out of my wits. What should I do?"

"Now listen, Debbie, and listen very carefully. You're going to be all right—if you play it smart."

Now what did he mean by that?

"I'm trying to, Steve. But he's called three times now. The last time I was afraid it was you, and I knew I'd better answer it. If I didn't answer, you would have thought I had left the apartment. I didn't want to disappoint you."

"You're a good girl, Debbie, and you haven't disappointed me. Here's what we're going to do. I'm going to call you at nine in the morning, at noon, at three in the afternoon, and at six in the evening. That's every three hours beginning at nine and ending at six. That should be easy to remember."

"Okay, I got that."

"Now, if the telephone rings at any other time, don't answer it. I mean, *don't* answer it. And, Debbie, whatever you do, if someone comes to the door, don't answer that either!"

It all sounded so ominous.

"Steve," I blurted out, "I'm deathly afraid! Are they really going to kill me?"

"Now, now, Debbie," he comforted, "don't go getting upset. Nobody's going to be able to touch you—if you do what I say."

Somehow he didn't sound all that reassuring. I suspect he was afraid himself.

"But, Steve, suppose they come to the hospital and finish you off? What then?"

"I don't think they know where I am. Maybe they think I'm in the apartment. Whatever you do, don't tell anyone where I am."

"But, Steve, why is my life being threatened? I didn't do anything to anyone. At least I don't think I did."

"Of course you didn't, Debbie. So don't be afraid. You're going to be okay. Just do what I say."

"I will, Steve, I will. But I sure don't like what's going on. I'm sure not going to sleep tonight!"

"Listen, sweetheart, we're going to get out of this all right, and we'll have a lot of fun together. I've been lying here thinking of all the fancy restaurants I'm going to take you to, and I plan to buy you some more clothes. I mean, really beautiful clothes! So you just hang in there, baby. In two or three days everything will pass. Why, we won't even know anything bad happened."

When we said good-bye, my mind was more on the terrifying situation than on fancy restaurants and high-fashion clothes. *What am I to do next?* I wondered. Should I call the police for my own protection?

I knew I couldn't do that. Steve was always so adamant about getting the police involved. Besides, I had a sneaking suspicion that whatever Steve was up to, it was on the wrong side of the law. I just couldn't figure it out. Why all this big money and expensive apartment? And why must everything be so secretive?

Just then the phone rang again, and I jumped sky high. I headed toward it without thinking. But just as

I got my hand on it, I jerked back. I almost forgot what Steve told me. It wasn't time for him to call.

The phone kept ringing and ringing and ringing. It seemed like it rang for fifteen minutes. Have you ever just listened to a phone ring like that? It was absolutely driving me crazy. When I couldn't take it any longer, I thought seriously about ripping it out from the wall. But then Steve couldn't reach me.

I finally piled blankets and pillows over the phone. That muffled the sound a little; but the phone still kept ringing.

When it finally stopped, I was so relieved. I started pulling the pillows and blankets off, but it started ringing again. This would drive me nuts! Back on went the pillows and blankets.

Then an idea hit me. As soon as whoever was ringing hung up, I'd call Steve. The ringing wasn't quite as long this time, and finally I was able to dial the hospital.

"Steve, this is Debbie again. The phone's been ringing and ringing and ringing and driving me crazy. Did you call?"

"No, Debbie. Remember what I said. I will call you at nine, twelve, three, and six. Just remember that."

"Yes, I know what you said, Steve. But this ringing telephone is driving me bananas. Every time it rings, I almost go through the ceiling. I even thought of calling the police for protection."

When He heard the word *police,* Steve was the one who hit the ceiling. "Debbie, don't ever, I mean, *don't ever* call the police."

Then his voice softened a little. "Sweetheart, I know this is a problem for you. How I wish I could be there with you right now to comfort you. But there's one thing I absolutely can't have, and that's the police involved. I know who the guys are who did me in and are calling you. As soon as I get out of here, I'll take care of things my own way. If you call the police, they'll spoil it for me."

So that was it. Steve was already planning on revenge!

"Steve, here's my idea. I'm going to leave the phone off the hook until the times when you said you would call. That way the phone won't keep ringing and driving me crazy."

"Good idea! Leave the phone off the hook, and just stay cool. I just know everything is going to be all right."

When I told Steve good-bye, I hung up the receiver. But as soon as I did, I pulled it off again. Then I had peace and quiet.

About two minutes before the time Steve had said he would call, I replaced the receiver, and right on the button he called me.

He was feeling much stronger now. The doctor had said he would have to be in the hospital for another three weeks. But Steve told the doctor he would be out in three days! That would be Sunday.

Steve said the doctor really put up a fight over that, but finally admitted he couldn't keep him there against his wishes. As a compromise, Steve agreed to go into the doctor's office every day for a few weeks.

Saturday came, and I was anxiously awaiting Steve's homecoming. Besides, then I'd be able to get out of the apartment too. Even though it was beautiful, it was beginning to get on my nerves. My confinement here was making me more and more irritable—especially after those two years of being used to lots of fresh air and sunshine at the Greens.

The Greens! I wondered how they were getting along. They never would have believed the way I was able to make it on my own in New York City. I sure wasn't like all those other runaways everybody had warned me about!

I watched a lot of television while I sat there without anything else to do—soap operas, game shows, anything. At least it kept my mind off those sinister phone calls.

Around four Saturday afternoon I was startled as someone knocked on the apartment door. Maybe it was Steve. Maybe he got out early! But as I bounded toward the door in excitement, I remembered his warning, "Whatever you do, don't let anyone into the apartment!"

There was another loud bang at the door just as I reached it. Talk about hitting the ceiling! Wow! When I gained my composure, I looked through the little peephole in the door. Standing there were two police officers.

I breathed a sigh of relief. Now I wouldn't have to disobey Steve by calling them; they had come to me! But then I thought of the mysterious things Steve was doing. Had they come to arrest him? And if they did, would I be held as an accomplice?

As I was watching them, one of them banged on the door again with his nightstick—louder and more persistent this time. What was I going to do?

Just then one of them called, "This is the police. Don't be afraid. There has been a murder committed in this apartment house, and we have to talk to all the tenants. Would you mind opening the door so we can ask a few questions?"

A murder? I sure wasn't involved in that. This was going to be easy. Besides, I'd really be in trouble if I didn't cooperate. It didn't really occur to me that they had no way of knowing whether or not anyone was in the apartment.

So I unlatched the two bolts and unlocked the door. The two police officers were certainly big, but they weren't very handsome. In fact, they seemed downright ugly. I'd heard about people being afraid of the police in New York City. Well, these two ugly brutes would scare anyone to death. But then, I didn't think they chose police officers on the basis of their looks.

As they stepped toward the door, one of them said, "Do you mind if we come in and ask you a few questions?"

"Sure, it's okay. Come on in."

They moved on into the room, and I turned my back as I shut the door. The next thing I knew a great big hand was clamped over my mouth, and the officer said, "Shut up, kid, or this is going to be the end of you!"

That voice! It was the man who had been calling on the telephone!

Or was it just my imagination? I had to admit that it had been working overtime these past few days.

The officer dragged me into the middle of the room, pushed me into a chair, and demanded, "Okay, where is the cocaine stashed?"

What was this, a drug bust?

He lifted his hand from my mouth, and I said, "I thought you were police officers investigating a murder. What do you mean, where is the cocaine stashed?"

One of them slapped me across the face with the back of his hand. "Listen, kid, when I ask something, I expect a straight answer. Now tell me where it is before I hit you again!"

"Hey," I yelled back, "I heard about corruption in the police department, but I never expected to see it like this!"

His hand stung my face again. "Like I tell you, keep your big fat mouth shut! We're not police officers. This is the only way we could get into this apartment building."

Then he began to cuss. Yes, it *was* that man who had been calling me. I recognized the tone of his voice— and the awful words he was using.

The other guy put his hands around my throat and pulled me up. "Okay, kid, start chirping like a good little bird and tell us where the cocaine is stashed."

"Listen, you jerks," I yelled, "I don't know what you are talking about. So let me tell you, and tell you straight. I don't know too much about the guy who lives here. The only thing I know is that he picked me up on the street a little over a week ago, and I've been living here since then. He's got a lot of money, and he takes me to expensive places. He claims he's a sales-man. So help me, that's all I know. As far as any co-caine is concerned, I'm going to tell you the truth. I snorted some for the first time the other day, and I smoked a joint. That's all the drugs I know anything about."

One of them slapped me again. Oh, how it stung! I felt my cheek starting to swell. The whole picture sud-denly became clearer. Steve must be a drug pusher. That's where the sales came in.

How in the world did I ever get myself into this crazy

mess? If I couldn't tell these bums where the cocaine was, they would probably kill me. Why, oh why, didn't I stay upstate where I at least was safe?

The guy who had his hands around my throat pushed me back into the chair. Then he turned to his partner and said, "Well, what do you think? Shall we rape her now or later?"

I stiffened and screamed, "No! No! Please don't do that to me. Please! Please!"

They both laughed. "Well," one of them said, "it will be hard passing up an opportunity like this; but if you tell us where the cocaine is, kid, you'll stay a virgin for the rest of your life!"

What did he mean by that? Were they planning to kill me?

"Listen, gentlemen, please listen to me," I begged. "Do I have to repeat my story? I don't know where any cocaine is. Honest I don't."

"Well, Vincent," one of them said, "maybe if we fill the bathtub with water and tie her up in it, she'll start talking. If she doesn't, that's her tough luck. We can just leave her there to drown." Then to emphasize his point, he looked at me and asked, "Can you imagine what it feels like to have your hands and feet tied and be thrown into a bathtub face down? And the water slowly, slowly comes up, and you drown. Real slow. I understand it's an absolutely horrible way to die!"

I began trembling from head to toe. Would these men really do something like this to me? If they were the ones who almost killed Steve—and somehow I knew they were—they wouldn't stop at anything!

Just then one of them grabbed the front of my blouse and ripped it off. He forced my hands behind my back, stood me up, and trussed me up like a chicken. Was he going to carry out his threat?

"Listen, kid, I'm going to give you one more chance. Either you start chirping, or you're going to get it both ways. First we'll rape you, and then we'll throw you into the tub to drown!"

I started to bawl like a baby. "Please! Please!" I whimpered. "I don't know how to get this across to you. I don't have the slightest idea where any cocaine is. All I know is that I was sitting here in the living room, and Steve went back toward his bedroom and came back with two packets. That's all I know."

Vincent threw me to the floor roughly, pulled some tape from his pocket, and taped my legs together with row after row of tape. "Now, kid, you just lay there on the floor and don't try to go anywhere," he ordered. "If you start to scream, I'll stomp your tongue out with my boots!"

The other fellow, whom he called Joe, had already started down the hall to Steve's bedroom, and Vincent followed him as soon as he was convinced I was securely tied.

I could hear them smashing things all over the place. That must be the bed they knocked over. Ripping, slashing, breaking, crashing. They must have turned every drawer upside down on the floor. Then it sounded like the dresser went over. Glass smashed. They were so frantic that they weren't about to stop at anything. I wondered if they were slashing Steve's expensive paintings. What was he was going to say when he came home tomorrow and found this horrible mess? And me dead!

They must have searched every inch of that bedroom and apparently they didn't find anything, for they stomped back out into the living room.

"Listen, kid, not a thing anywhere in there. If you're lying to us, it's going to be all over for you. You sure you're telling the truth?"

"Yes, I'm telling the truth!" I screamed.

Vincent turned to Joe and said, "Joe, I know that Steve DiSilva has a stash somewhere. Alonzo told me he saw him buying the big package. There has to be two million bucks worth of cocaine stashed somewhere in this apartment. Now where do you think he could possibly hide it?"

Two million bucks worth? Wow! Steve really was a big-time dealer. No wonder he was so worried about his apartment. So help me, if he had leveled with me and told me what he was doing, I never would have gotten myself into this mess. But where would I have gone? Probably some pimp would have me by now!

Vincent yelled again, "Joe, it's just got to be in this apartment! Come on! Let's take it apart!"

Like two maniacs they began ripping and slashing the sofa and chairs. They pulled down all the paintings and slashed them. They dumped out all the potted plants. Then they stormed into my bedroom and devastated it. Then the kitchen. They must have even pushed over the refrigerator. I heard pots and pans banging. And their voices got louder and louder and their curses worse and worse as they got more and more frustrated.

They went into the bathroom and knocked everything off every shelf and turned over every planter. I guess there wasn't an inch of that apartment where they didn't look.

When they came stomping back into the living

room, the whole beautiful apartment looked like a tenement shack. I've never seen anything in shambles like it was. By this time the two thugs were raving mad.

Vincent grabbed me and lifted me straight up off the floor. "Listen, kid, maybe you're telling the truth, and maybe you're not. But, Joe, let's get something out of this anyway!"

Here it was coming! Rape!

I stiffened and yelled, "No! No! Don't try anything, please! Please don't! I've told you all I know."

"I still think we ought to drown her," Joe said. "I can't stand snotty broads like her."

"No! No! Please believe me!" I begged. "I had absolutely nothing to do with Steve's business dealings. And as soon as you guys leave, I'm on my way. I'm getting out of this mess!"

Vincent slapped me across the face again—this time so hard I could taste blood. "Shut up!" he screamed. "I've had enough of your lip! I still think you know where that cocaine is stashed."

"Okay, kill me!" I screamed. "Do anything you want to me! But I don't know where any cocaine is! If I did, I'd tell you! I got nothing to lose by telling you. All I want is to get out of this place and go home. I'm a runaway from upstate New York, and I just want to get out of here!"

Both of them laughed uproariously. "Wow!" Vincent said. "When you squeal, you really squeal. You must have been raised with the pigs!"

By this time I was sobbing so hard that I couldn't get out another word. Vincent grabbed me up, threw me into one of Steve's antique chairs, and took some wire and tied me to it. My hands were still tied behind me, and my feet were secured with tape. Then he went to the bathroom, got one of those plush towels, and tied it around my mouth so hard that I could scarcely breathe.

"All right, kid," Vincent said as he got right down into my face, "maybe you don't know where the stuff is stashed. Maybe Joe and me are being softer than we should. We're going to give you a break; but, remember, when old lover boy comes home and finds you, you don't know what happened. Here's your story. You opened the door for a couple of cops, and somebody hit you over the head. You didn't get a chance to see anybody or hear anything. Right?"

I nodded my head vigorously. I wasn't about to disagree with them on anything!

"Oh," Joe said, "look here! Your telephone is off the hook! Did you know that? Maybe that explains the busy signals, Vincent. Well, let us be gentlemen and replace it for you. Maybe someone will want to call you!" Then he laughed uproariously at his own joke.

They headed toward the door, carefully closing it behind them. I knew they didn't want any of the other tenants finding me.

When I was sure they weren't coming back, I tried jerking my hands and legs to free them. They were tied fast.

I tried to yell. But no words came out—only sounds muffled by a thick, luxurious towel that once I thought felt so heavenly.

I kept squirming and twisting, but nothing would budge. Now I was really scared. Was I going to have to stay like this until Steve got home tomorrow? And what if the doctor reconsidered and wouldn't let him come home yet? Would I die here? What a horrible death! It would be worse than drowning!

Why did this have to happen to me? I was just an innocent little runaway taken in by a big-time drug dealer. Do all runaways get into trouble like this in New York City?

I glanced at the clock. Two minutes before six. Time for Steve to call. At least the phone was on the hook. But how could I ever get over there to answer it?

7

As the clock chimed six, the phone began to ring. Just like Steve. Right on time. But how was I going to tell him about my predicament? The chair where I was tied was quite a distance from the phone, and even if I could get over there, how could I pick up the receiver with my hands tied? Or how could I talk with that towel around my mouth?

Maybe if somehow I could get over there and knock off the receiver and mumble something, he'd know there was a problem. Maybe he had a friend he could call to come and help me. Or did drug dealers trust anybody?

I raised up off the seat of the chair slightly, and the chair came up with me. Fortunately it wasn't a very heavy chair, so I could rock back and forth. That plush carpet impeded my progress. This would have been a lot easier on a bare floor! Now if Steve wouldn't hang up.

By raising slightly and shuffling along, I was able to move the chair toward the phone. Good! I was almost there. But how was I going to nudge that receiver off? Certainly not with my hands. Maybe I could nudge my head against it.

I kept shifting around until I was right up next to the phone. Now for the nudge. I lunged toward the receiver—and missed! I tumbled to the floor, still bound in the chair, my feet in the air. I struggled to turn over. No way. I was jammed against the wall.

All this time the phone kept ringing and ringing. Then silence. I had failed. Big tears welled up in my eyes. I felt so alone—and so terrified. That was his last call for the day!

How in the world was I going to get back up? Now I had to be especially careful of the telephone cord, for if I knocked off the receiver now and Steve got a busy signal, he would think I had taken the receiver off deliberately.

The more I struggled, the more tired and frustrated I got. My energy just seemed to drain from me, and I hurt in every part of my body.

I just had to get upright again. I kept pushing and nudging with my toes. My hands seemed a little looser with all my struggles, so I could use them a little too. But I had to aim myself away from the telephone lest I knock off the receiver prematurely.

Then I gave one extra hard push, and I was upright again. The chair teetered back and forth a few times, but it didn't fall over. Now I was shedding tears of relief.

Exhausted, I looked back at the clock. Eight forty-five. Would Steve try again in fifteen minutes, or would I have to wait until morning?

The minutes ticked by as I maneuvered the chair over by the phone. If that phone rang, I sure was going to try again!

One minute till nine. Then the clock started to

chime. Sure enough, the telephone rang. It must be Steve!

This time I was going to be more careful. I began to rock the chair back and forth, very carefully aiming my head toward the receiver. At just the right moment I would lunge. I struggled against the towel.

One more rocking back and forth should do it. But just before I started to lunge, I heard a loud crack! I collapsed to the floor.

Oh, why did they have to tie me up in an antique chair! One of those stupid legs broke under me!

As I lay there cursing to myself, I struggled, but I was hopelessly bound. Even if I could get upright, the chair wouldn't hold me now.

The phone kept ringing and ringing and ringing. I lay there so frustrated. I knew it was useless to try anything else. The phone rang for at least ten minutes. And that ringing above my ear was excruciating!

I tried to scream, but no sound came out. I tried kicking, but my feet were still bound. I jerked my shoulders around to try to get free from the wires around my wrists, but they just cut deeper. What was I going to do now? I knew my struggle was hopeless. I was so exhausted that I didn't feel like moving at all. Maybe this was the way I was going to die!

I tried to sleep as the moments ticked by. Time seemed endless. I forced myself not to think of how hungry I was or how much I needed to go to the bathroom. But the more I tried not to think about those things, the more I thought about them.

The clock chimed midnight. Every bone in my body ached. I squirmed and wriggled and—

Just then I heard it—the door. Oh, no! Those animals hadn't locked it behind them—only closed it, and they were coming back to finish me off!

The front door opened, and a light flipped on. Then I heard loud cursing. I recognized that voice! Steve!

I tried to yell, but not much sound could get through that towel. I made as much noise as I could, and I heard Steve's footsteps hurrying my way.

When he saw me, he shouted, "Debbie! Debbie! What happened?"

Couldn't he see that I couldn't talk? He did, and he bent down and untied the gag. "Debbie, what has happened to this apartment? Tell me!"

"Steve, you'll never believe what I've been through. Two guys dressed like cops came in here and tore this place to shreds, looking for cocaine."

"Cocaine? Don't tell me they did this to my beautiful apartment just to get a bag of cocaine? I don't have any cocaine here. The only cocaine I've had recently were those packets that you and I snorted your first night here."

"Steve, please untie me. I've got no feeling in my legs and arms."

His hands trembled as he began to undo the wire and tape. "I just absolutely can't believe this," he was saying over and over. "Why would two cops come in here and tear this apartment up this way? So help me, if I ever find out who those guys were, I'm going to kill them!"

Finally he had me untied, and I sat there rubbing my arms and legs and hands and feet until they began to tingle.

But what about Steve? Was he telling the truth? And why was he more concerned over his apartment than over what had happened to me?

"Steve, this whole thing was a nightmare," I started. "I let them in because they said they were cops investigating a murder in this building. But they weren't cops. One of them was the guy who has been calling here. They did almost everything imaginable to get information out of me about cocaine. They claimed you've got two million bucks worth. They threatened to rape me. And to drown me. It was horrible!"

"Yeah, but what about my apartment?" Steve countered. "They have totally devastated this place. It'll cost me thousands of dollars to get it back where it was before!"

We walked from room to room surveying the damage. Steve was obviously weak from his hospitalization. And now this! I thought he was going to cry, but he stood in the middle of the mess and yelled, "So help me, if I ever find out who did this, the city morgue will be taking care of two new corpses!"

"Should we call the real police?" I asked.

"No! No!" he shouted. No matter what happens to us, we never, never call the police!"

That was more than I could take. "Steve," I screamed, "I'm heading back upstate. I've had enough of the city. I've had enough of fancy clothes and restaurants. Enough of drugs." Then I looked him squarely in the eye. "And, Steve, I've had enough of you!"

I turned and headed for the door. I knew I was in terrible shape, but I had to get out of here now!

Steve ran after me and grabbed my arm. "Please, Debbie, calm down. You can't go out there at midnight looking like that. Besides, can't you understand my predicament? So help me, I have no idea what those guys were after. It could very possibly be a case of mistaken identity. Everything I do is legitimate. I didn't want to tell you this, but the reason I have so much money is that I received an enormous inheritance from my father. I'm a graduate of Harvard and majored in business and have made some fantastic investments. I'm so wealthy that I don't have to work. I know the sales bit was a lie, but, Debbie, I had to see if I could trust you. I didn't want someone running after me just for my money!"

I felt so foolish. Here Steve had almost lost his life. Now when he returned to his apartment because he was worried about me, he was devastated by the enormous damage. And to think I didn't care!

This wealthy young man had picked me up off the street and shared his life with me, expecting nothing in return. I walked over and tenderly hugged him. "Steve," I said, "I'm sorry for the way I acted. I had no idea what your background was."

He put his arms around me and drew me close. "Well, Debbie, I really wasn't ready yet to say too much about my past. I've been called a lot of dirty names just because I happened to be born into an extremely wealthy family. Some people suffer from being poor; I suffered from being rich. But at least I had enough sense to get a good education and do something with the investments."

Just then the telephone rang. I tensed, and I could feel Steve's body tense too. "Who in the world is that?" I asked.

"I don't know," Steve replied, worry cresting on his forehead. "Especially at this hour of the night!"

"You think it's those two hoods again?" I asked. "They might be checking to see if anyone has discovered yet what they've done."

"Well, it could be the hospital," Steve said. "I had to bribe an orderly to get my clothes and money and let me out. They weren't going to dismiss me until tomorrow, but I was frantic when I couldn't reach you on the phone. I knew something was up."

"Yeah, that's it," I responded. "It's the hospital. So let's just let it ring."

"Yes, but it might be somebody else," Steve said. "I think I'd better answer it."

"But, Steve," I protested, "suppose it is those two thugs. They said they were the ones who had stabbed you. If they know you're here, they might decide to come back and finish you off."

Apparently that didn't worry Steve, for he went in and picked up the phone. He stood there listening for several minutes and finally said, "Hey, man, everything's cool. Don't worry about one little thing. You'll get your money; I promise." Then he hung up.

All this just didn't fit together. If Steve were into investments, why were people calling him at one in the morning for money? Was Steve really telling me the truth about his past?

"Well, Debbie, I guess we might as well clean up this place the best we can," and he started to straighten a few chairs.

"Steve, we're both exhausted. Let's do the bulk of the straightening tomorrow. For now, let's just clean up enough so we can have a place to sleep." With that I headed for his bedroom and started shoving some of the big pieces of furniture back into place. Then I had to go to the bathroom.

I stepped inside his bathroom and closed the door, but didn't lock it. After all, he was at the other end of the apartment. Or so I thought.

Then I head him yell, "Debbie, where are you?"

"In your bathroom, Steve. My kidneys are so full that they started to run over!"

Then I heard him running. He hit the bathroom door full force and screamed, "What are you doing in here?"

"Steve, get out of here!" I yelled. "I'm going to the bathroom!"

I was embarrassed enough to have him come barging in. But the next thing I knew he had grabbed me, screaming, "Girl, I don't mind your living with me, but there is absolutely no way that you're ever going to use my bathroom!"

I was trying to pull my pants up and wasn't prepared for the back of his hand which whacked my face.

I backed away. "Steve, for crying out loud, what is with you? You think I'm full of venereal disease, don't you?"

"No, that's not the problem. I just don't want anyone else using my bathroom."

"Steve, I can't imagine your acting spoiled like that. You've shared everything with me. But now you're acting like a little brat just because I was using your bathroom. What gives?"

"Like I tell you," he sulked, "I don't want anyone else using my bathroom."

I walked down the hall to the other bathroom. This time I not only made sure the door was closed behind me, but also bolted!

Later I walked back out into the hallway so confused. Something was terribly wrong with this setup. Things just didn't add up. And I figured I'd better get to the bottom of things while I still could.

I went to my bedroom and started pulling my

clothes out of the closet. Steve walked in and asked, "What's going on?"

"Steve," I said, "it's for sure this time. I've just got to leave. I don't understand what's going on around here, and I'm scared to death. I almost died for you, and then you slap me around for a major offense like using your bathroom. Then that telephone call. I'm sorry, but I'm on my way."

He stared at me. "You're not going to the police, are you?"

"I might."

"Debbie, what will it take for you not to go to the police?"

"What do you mean, what will it take?"

"I mean, how much money can I give you for you to keep your mouth shut? You quote a price, and I'll see if I can give it to you. Then you can go on your way and go home."

Now I knew Steve was lying about his past. What was he really up to? And why was it so important that I not go to the police?

"Listen, Steve, when those two guys were here tearing this place apart, they were convinced that you are a cocaine dealer. Are you?"

He looked at me; then he started to study the floor, avoiding my gaze. I knew I had him.

"Listen, Steve, you don't need to tell me anything more. You're a dealer, so why don't you admit it? In fact, if you don't admit it, it won't make any difference. You're still a dealer."

He stalked away, and I kept packing.

In a few minutes he came back and stood in the doorway. "Okay, Debbie, have it your way. I'm a dealer."

"Steve, that kind of life can get you killed."

"Well, that's the risk you have to take. Look at this beautiful apartment. I mean, obviously not at this moment, but at the way it's been. I have fancy clothes and can go out to expensive restaurants and have a good-looking girl like you. I didn't tell you this, but I have a Rolls-Royce. I keep it in the garage."

"But, Steve, it's against the law to sell drugs. One day you're going to get caught, and you can get life imprisonment. I mean, is it worth it?"

He laughed. "I'm willing to take the chance."

"What about those two thugs who came here and tore this place apart?" I asked. "Who were they, anyway?"

"They're some other dealers. You see, dealers don't really like each other. They'll kill to get drugs. They know I got a $2 million shipment and suspected I had it here in my apartment. But I sure fooled them." He grinned.

"What do you mean, fooled them? They tore up every inch of this beautiful apartment! They would have found any cocaine if it had been here."

"Wrong! Come on, Debbie. I want to show you something."

He led me down the hall and into his bathroom. I tensed as we got to the door.

"The reason I didn't want you in here," he started, "was that I was afraid you might find something. And the same reason I didn't want to tell you what was going on was that I was afraid that those other dealers might bust in here. If you knew where the drugs were hidden, you might have given in to their torture. Those two guys cut me up, trying to make me tell them where the stuff was hidden. But I told them if they killed me, they never would know; so they didn't go quite that far. That's why they left me alive. But I really outfoxed them this time. Look at where I've got it hidden."

Steve took the roll of toilet paper out of the roller. Then he reached inside the roll and pushed a little button. The side of the roll fell off. Inside were packets and packets of cocaine!

"This is the real stuff," he said proudly. "Two million dollars worth."

My mouth flew open. I couldn't believe it.

"And, Debbie, that's why I didn't want you using my bathroom. As you pulled the paper off, you might have heard something rattle in there and began to inspect it. That might have revealed the hiding place."

Clever! People tearing apart an apartment wouldn't look in the toilet paper!

Steve carefully replaced the edge of the toilet-paper roll. It was disguised so perfectly. The outer edge looked just like paper.

"Where did you get something like that?" I asked.

"There's a Japanese craftsman here in the city who makes all sorts of things out of plastic. He makes those imitation dishes of food that stores use for their displays. I explained to him what I needed, and he was a master at it. I told him it was where I was going to hide my jewels. He made a perfect replica of a roll of toilet paper. Fantastic idea, right?"

I just stood there looking at $2 million worth of cocaine. I couldn't even imagine that kind of money.

"Let me show you something else," Steve said.

He led me back into the living room where he reached for the mantel clock. As he picked it up, he pushed the wood on the end. There were three pistols.

As he showed them to me, he said, "I don't like to do this, but I guess I'm going to have to start carrying a gun because of those two characters. The problem with carrying a gun is that you might be stopped by the cops and arrested for possession of firearms without a permit. These cops are very smart. They may know a guy is a dealer, but they also know they're probably not going to have enough evidence to get him on drug charges. So they look for other ways to bust the guy. Piddling little things like speeding tickets. Or income tax evasion charges. What they are trying to do is put the guy in prison, and they'll do whatever they have to, to get him out of circulation. So even if they suspect me for dealing in drugs, they'll try to get me on other technicalities.

"But right now I'm going to lay low. If those two thugs try anything again, I'm going to knock both of them off!"

"You mean you'd kill those two guys?"

"You'd better believe it. Before they killed me."

"Or me," I added.

Steve smiled. "You catch on quickly. Maybe you should carry a gun too."

Steve pulled one of the guns out of the clock and handed it to me. "It's loaded!" he warned. "Don't monkey with the trigger."

The steel felt so cold and uncomfortable. I quickly handed the gun back to him and said, "No thanks. I think I'd better take my chances."

Steve slipped the gun into his pocket. "Now, Debbie, if anything like this ever happens again, you know where the guns are. If someone knocks at the door and you aren't sure who it is, come here and get a gun first.

Next time you might not be as lucky as you were this time."

I wasn't about to forget that. And I wasn't going to be tied up again. Ever!

We straightened up the bedrooms, and since it was so late, and we were both exhausted, he suggested we get some sleep.

The next couple of weeks we spent cleaning up the mess those two thugs had left in the apartment. Steve replaced some of the pieces that were too badly damaged to repair. And every once in a while I noticed him going into his bathroom to get drugs to sell.

He told me he kept the bulk of his money in a bank. But, of course, he couldn't keep his cocaine there.

We kept snorting—more and more frequently. I noticed Steve was getting high quite a few times a day, and he'd always ask me to join him. I guess that's one of the reasons Steve wanted me around. I was someone he could share things with.

One afternoon he gave me twenty dollars and sent me after some groceries we needed. He seemed agitated, restless.

I spent almost fifteen dollars for what we needed. When I turned the corner and headed toward the entrance of our apartment, I saw four police cars out in front. Their red lights blinked eerily. What could have happened?

I was almost at the front door when cops started pouring out of the building. Then I looked, astonished. There was Steve, handcuffed, between two plainclothes detectives. When he saw me, he shook his head in a warning. I stood there, frozen in my tracks.

More policemen poured out of the building. Then

more detectives. One detective carried a roll of toilet paper. Someone had discovered Steve's secret!

As I stared at the evidence the cops had, I knew that my life in Steve's apartment had come to an end. I wasn't about to go back inside that building. They would get me too.

So, I turned and headed down the street. All I had for the days I spent with Steve were the clothes I was wearing, a bag of groceries, and a five-dollar bill.

Where was I going to go now? And what was I going to do?

8 I quickened my pace as I moved away from Steve DiSilva's Central Park West apartment. I had enjoyed luxury I didn't know existed, while I lived with that drug dealer. But he was on his way to prison now. Of that I was sure. And I didn't want those cops grabbing me. I knew I'd get at least fifteen years as an accomplice, and I wasn't about to go to prison.

I cut through Central Park and ended up on the Avenue of the Americas. Since there were a lot of people moving around, I felt more secure.

A few blocks later I stopped in front of the Hilton hotel. The walk had been brisk, and I was tired. I looked inside and saw the plush seats in the cocktail lounge. It hadn't taken me long to get accustomed to nice things. So I thought, *Why not go inside and rest?* After all, I could get my head together and figure out what to do next. I had only five dollars—and nowhere to spend the night!

It felt so good just to sit down. My legs ached. In a

few moments a cocktail waitress asked if I wanted a drink. "No thanks," I told her, "I'm just waiting for my dad. We're staying here at the hotel, and I'm supposed to meet him here."

She smiled and moved on. I knew she didn't believe my story. But if she only knew!

A little later a man I would estimate to be about forty sat down in a chair opposite me. "Can I buy you a drink?" he asked as he smiled.

Should I tell him the same story I told the waitress? No, not this time. After all, maybe it would relax me if I had a drink.

"Yes, that would be nice," I said as I returned his smile.

In a few moments when the cocktail waitress returned, she said, "So this is your father, huh? Well, you've certainly got a good-looking father!"

Now what was I going to do? I couldn't tell her she was wrong.

The guy looked at the waitress and grinned. "Don't you think I have a better looking daughter?" he asked.

Hey! This was going to be easier than I thought!

I ordered a screwdriver, and the guy ordered a martini. I'm sure the waitress wondered if I were too young, but she looked sort of dumb—and I sure wasn't worried about it.

When she left, the guy leaned over and half-whispered, "My name is Oscar Winowitz."

"Oscar what?" I asked with a chuckle.

"Yeah, I know. I can't help the name. Here, I'll spell it for you: W-i-n-o-w-i-t-z."

"Oh, I get it."

"And what's your name?" he asked.

Should I tell him? I sized him up as harmless and answered, "Debbie Carter."

He reached across and took my hand tenderly. Then with his other hand he began to pat it. "Nice name, Debbie. I'm sure glad to meet you."

"Thanks. Glad to meet you too."

"What brings you to the big city?" Oscar wanted to know.

"Oh, my dad and I came from Chicago. He's at a business meeting, and I'm waiting for him. He should be here in a couple of minutes."

"Oh, that's nice. Been here long?"

"No, just two days. Kind of a dumpy city, if you ask me."

Oscar laughed. "Yeah, I know. But they have some cute-looking chicks who come in and out of the city. I mean, you know, like you."

I snickered at his obvious compliment. "Well, Oscar, I have a boyfriend back in Chicago. He wants me to marry him before too long."

"Oh, that's nice. By the way, how old are you?"

Why was this guy asking so many personal questions? And to ask my age seemed a little too personal. But he had bought me a drink.

"Twenty-one," I lied.

"Do you go out?" he asked.

"What do you mean, do I go out? I just told you I have a boyfriend."

He leaned closer and whispered, "I mean, why don't you come up to my room? I'll make it worth your while."

I stood in shock. This was the first time in my life I had been propositioned, and it made me angry. I certainly didn't look like a prostitute, did I?

He also stood up. "Now, now, Debbie, calm down. Just sit down and play it cool."

"Listen, you jerk," I said, "I'm not that kind of a girl. My dad is going to be along here in a couple of minutes. If you don't keep your big fat mouth shut, I'll call the cops and have you arrested."

"Oh, is that right?" he responded. "You're going to have me busted, huh? I mean, like put me away for twenty years?"

"Well, I don't know how long they put away men like you for, but don't you dare try anything like that again!"

Just then the cocktail waitress walked up with our drinks. Oscar pulled out a wad of bills. He paid her and gave her a big tip. The guy must be rich.

As we started sipping our drinks, Oscar leaned closer again. Somehow I suspected that behind that smiling face was somebody else.

"Come on, Debbie; what do you think? Don't jump up this time. Like I say, I'll make it worth your while."

This character was so insistent. How could I get rid of him? But then where was I going to go?

Then Oscar whispered, "I have a son about your age, I think. His name is Steve DiSilva."

I jerked back and stared. Don't tell me that my boy-friend Steve had this creep as a father? Then it hit me. This guy had told me his name was Oscar Winowitz. How could he be the father of Steve DiSilva? Fathers and sons have the same last name.

When I asked him about that inconsistency, he leaned forward and whispered again, "Debbie, don't you know who I am? Don't you remember me?"

I jerked back and stared. So help me, as far as I knew, I had never seen this guy in my whole life.

"I'm sorry, Oscar, but I don't know who you are."

"Debbie, I was one of Steve's regular customers. I don't know how much cocaine I've bought from him, but it's been a lot. And I've seen you with him quite a number of times. I know you're Steve's girl."

So that was it. This guy was a user. I wondered if he knew about Steve getting busted. Was that why he was trying to muscle in?

As if to answer my question, he went on, "And I'll bet you hardly have a penny on you, do you? I mean, after they just got Steve and all. You were lucky to get out of there."

So Oscar knew. But how did he know so quickly?

Well, Oscar kept persisting. He kept bargaining. And the price got higher and higher. I was absolutely broke and had to have some money, so I swallowed my pride and was finally forced to say yes—to survive.

We finished our drinks and headed toward the elevators. "Let's walk up," he suggested. "I don't want anybody following." Then as we started up the stairs, he said, "Your friend Steve had the best cocaine in town. Too bad he got busted."

"Yeah, I know. Not only did Steve get busted, but my world just came to an end."

"Oh, Debbie, with your good looks, you'll be okay. I mean, you got all it takes to make a lot of money."

I knew he was talking about my becoming a prostitute, but I wasn't interested. This would be the last time. As soon as I got enough money, I was going to try to get out of town—maybe even go back to the Greens.

As we reached the second floor, he led me down a hallway. Then he turned to me and said, "Debbie, I hate to tell you this, but I'm a cop, a detective from the vice squad."

I jumped back, but he grabbed my wrist and held on tight. "Now cool it," he said; "don't get so excited."

This guy couldn't be for real. "Oscar," I said, "you're the funniest guy I've ever met. I don't understand what this is about, but I don't believe you're a cop. So quit trying to scare me."

He reached into his coat pocket and flipped out his badge. Oh, no! He *was* a cop! A New York City Police Department detective!

Suddenly the pieces fit together. When I took off, Oscar must have tailed me. He didn't have any proof to tie me to drugs, so he had carefully set up a situation to arrest me on prostitution charges. It was like Steve said: If they can't get you on one charge, they'll try to get you on another.

I was just about to tell this dirty old man what I thought of his plan to arrest me, when he said, "Debbie, here's the deal. We go to my room, and it's free. No arrest. Free for me and freedom for you. Is it a deal?"

I tried to stare a hole through him. This was absolutely disgusting.

"Of course it's no deal, you filthy louse!" I exploded.

"Hey, stay cool, will you?" Oscar said, giving my arm a slight twist to try to calm me down. "You've got to learn the game. And if you learn the game right, then you'll stay out of a peck of trouble. And if you don't play it right, I'm probably going to find your body in a back alley someplace. There's a lot of perverts down there on the streets, so you've got to be wise to the streets. Now come on to my room, and I'll give you a few lessons on how to stay alive."

In his room Oscar explained to me all about being a prostitute. He told me you always get the money first. Then he told me always to carry a switchblade. I had goofed up on the first part of that advice, but I was way ahead on the second.

Then he told me to get in contact with the girls in the street and find out immediately who the perverts were—and the decoy cops. He told me the police will put their own women on the streets to look like prostitutes, but they're really cops. Guys come up to them and get the shock of their lives! And jail too!

Then Oscar told me to be careful where I went with the guys, or "johns," as they were referred to by the girls. He gave me the names of a couple of hotels and told me how to approach the guy at at the desk. I could usually work a deal with them, he said, and give them part of my earnings.

Oscar spent a long time telling me about pimps. Watch out for those guys, he warned. It was very rare that any of them would ever treat a girl right. I'd be better off by myself, he said.

Oscar told me the girls usually hung around the cocktail lounges or stood in front of the hotels. Many guys come to the city looking for girls. If I kept myself attractive, I'd never have any problem making good money, he said.

Then the subject of drugs came up. Oscar said he knew about Steve and had the apartment staked out for quite a long time. He had indeed tailed me from the apartment to the Hilton. He said he had been tempted to take me in, but he decided to let me go.

In fact, he said that when he walked into the cocktail

lounge, he had noticed two other girls sitting there. He asked if I noticed that when I came in, they got up and left.

As I tried to remember, I did recollect two good-looking girls getting up. They looked like airline stewardesses. Oscar told me they were prostitutes. He told me I could learn some things from them if I kept my ears open.

I don't know how long we spent talking, but Oscar gave me an education like I'd never had before. The sordid world of prostitution and drugs was devastating.

Then he encouraged me to get out of the city and go back home. I explained to him about the situation with the Greens. He thought I really ought to check to see if it had changed any.

Finally Oscar seemed to have said all he was planning to say on the subject of prostitution. We had talked so long that I thought he was just going to give me a lecture and let me go. I thought he'd forget that little deal he had suggested.

But no way. He insisted that we go through with it. Payment for information and for freedom, he laughingly called it.

When we got through, I felt so degraded and dehumanized. It was as though part of me had died. And to think I had to go through it and still didn't have any money!

I left his room and walked down the hall feeling absolutely terrible. But I also knew I was lucky I hadn't gotten busted. Right now I could be sitting in a dirty, filthy, rotten jail cell—instead of walking around in the Hilton hotel. So, in a way, maybe Oscar had done me a big favor.

I dragged down the steps and headed for the front door. Over to the right I saw the two girls sitting in the cocktail lounge. One of them motioned for me to come over. She looked harmless, so I sauntered over.

"Have a seat," one of them said.

I looked them over carefully. What did they want?

"Here, kid, sit down," she said again. "We've got a couple of lessons to teach you."

"Lessons? What do you mean, lessons? You don't even know me."

The other one laughed. "Maybe not, but we saw you walking off with Oscar Winowitz. And I don't think you were going upstairs to have a cup of tea with Oscar, were you?"

I felt so embarrassed. They knew what I had done.

"Here, kid, like I said, sit down."

I sat. The girls introduced themselves: Maria and Stephany. I told them my real name. I could see no point in pretense here.

"I suppose," Maria started in, "that you're relieved that Oscar didn't bust you and take you to jail, aren't you?"

"Yeah," I said. "Dumb me! The first guy I run into is a detective."

"You sure were up there a long time with him," Stephany said.

"Yeah, I know. Oscar told me about all that goes on in the street—how to protect myself and all that. I guess he felt sorry for me. Boy, was I ever lucky that time!"

"Did he show you his badge?" Maria asked.

"He sure did! Scared me to death!"

Then I said, "You girls sure seem to know a lot about Oscar. Has he ever busted you?"

"Naw, Oscar's never busted us," Stephany replied.

"Wow!" I said. "I guess you two have been lucky with the guy too. If you ask me, he makes a lousy detective."

"That's just it, Debbie," Maria said as kindly as she could. "Oscar's no detective!"

I stared at them unbelievingly. They weren't joking!

"What?" I responded in utter amazement. "Oscar's no detective?"

"Nope, he's not a detective!" Maria said with finality.

If Oscar weren't a detective, that meant that I let myself—The utter horror and stupidity of the situation was beginning to sink in.

"But," I protested, "the guy had a badge! I mean, I even saw it myself! He's a detective with the vice squad of the New York City Police Department."

Maria and Stephany were trying to be as kind to me as they knew how to be. "That's just it, Debbie," Maria said. "The guy is screwier than a bedbug. All of us girls know about Oscar. He always gets it free from the new girls."

"What?" I responded, still in shock over the situation. "What's his game?"

"Like I said," Maria went on, "the guy's a real nut. He lives in Los Angeles and comes to New York City about every other week. The guy's got money, but he never spends a dime on a girl. He's got this crazy thing about prostitutes and being a detective. About every other month, he seems to play this game where he buys a girl a drink, and then from there they go up to his room. Of course, he pulls his badge and gives them the big story about being a detective."

"Why, that dirty, filthy liar!" I exploded. "I ought to call the real cops and have him busted."

The girls laughed. "That's just it," Stephany said. "The cops wouldn't believe your story, and Oscar knows it. And in his own way he's harmless. He's not perverted—at least, not in the usual sense of that term. But the guy really knows about the world of prostitution."

"That's for sure!" I responded. "He gave me an education like I've never had before."

"It's the same old story," Maria said. "He has a knack for picking up new girls who usually have run away to the city. Then, the same old story. The cheapskate gets what he wants—for nothing."

Maria and Stephany seemed so understanding that I poured out the whole story of Steve's getting busted and my not having any place to go; and why I had been so ready to believe Oscar because he knew about Steve being busted and about my being Steve's girl.

Maria must have sensed my disillusionment and said, "Debbie, you look like a sweet kid. What do you say about Stephany and me kind of helping you out? We'll start by pointing out some of the people you need to stay away from."

Then they began to tell me about their lives. I just couldn't bear the thought of becoming a prostitute. But there seemed no way out for me now. Going back to the Greens was impractical and really unthinkable. This was where I had to stay—and what I had to do—whether I wanted to or not.

Maria and Stephany told me about the perverts and the decoys. They told me about using hotel rooms. They even walked with me to some of the hotels and introduced me to the desk clerks, told them what I was up to and that I would give part of the money to them.

I still felt so cheap and embarrassed by the whole thing.

The two were so helpful to me. They even invited me to share their apartment. It wasn't too bad; and since I had nowhere to go and no money, it made sense—at least for a while.

That evening the three of us headed back for the Hilton. Just as we started in the door, Maria grabbed my arm. "Don't go in there!" she cautioned. "The place is swarming with plainclothes detectives. Those four guys over there are from the vice squad."

I glanced over. They certainly didn't look like police officers to me; they looked like businessmen out to have a good time. But I knew Maria had been around long enough to know, and I trusted her.

We walked over to Forty-eighth and Broadway. It wasn't as good as the area around the Hilton. But it wasn't long before a guy came up to me and smiled. I asked him, "Want to go out?"

He nodded, and we headed for one of the hotels.

That night there were three men. I got through around one in the morning and headed back to the apartment. I felt absolutely horrible. I couldn't believe my dream was ending in shame this way.

I crawled into bed, but I couldn't sleep. I knew that I had died on the inside and had become a pawn for men's lusts. I wondered if a person could get any lower than I had, and I even contemplated suicide.

About three I heard Maria and Stephany come in all bubbly. "Hey, Debbie!" Maria called. "Have we ever got something for you!"

What could that be? I needed something, but most

of all I needed some sleep—and a clear conscience. I had neither.

Stephany went to the bathroom, came back, and sat on the sofa. Then she pulled a little white bag out of her bra and set the works on the table. They were going to shoot drugs.

"Ever snort cocaine?" I asked. It was the one drug I knew a little about.

"Yeah, a few times," Maria answered. "But heroin's the best. It lasts for a long time—not a flash like cocaine."

"Yeah, man, heroin's where it's at," Stephany chimed in.

They loaded the needle, and both of them got off.

"Here, let me get some for you," Maria suggested.

Something deep within me cried out to run. But I sat there and didn't even protest as Stephany made another fix.

"Ever use this before?" she asked.

I shook my head.

"Well, baby, one shot of this, and you've gone to heaven. I mean, it will feel real good!"

I extended my arm. Stephany was going to mainline. I looked at the needle and almost passed out on the spot. I turned my head the other way. The needle went in, and it hurt. I gritted my teeth.

Then it happened. It felt a little bit like cocaine, but it wasn't as quick a rush. And then it felt so good.

The three of us sat around nodding. We giggled and laughed. All the guilt of prostitution left my mind.

When I awoke the next day, I knew it was just the beginning. Already I had become a prostitute. I knew it wouldn't be long before I was a junkie. Never in my wildest moments had I thought it would end up this

way. I was Debbie Carter, and I was going to be different from all the other runaways. But here I was:
hooker and junkie. And it had happened so fast! Was
it all downhill from this point?

9 It didn't take long for me to get into the
vicious circle. I shot drugs when I got up, so I could
face going out on the street. After I got some money
and came back, I shot drugs so I could get to sleep.

I kept telling myself I only did this for fun—that I'd
never get hooked. But it wasn't too long before I had
to have more bags of heroin. Maybe I didn't admit it,
but I was hooked.

Maria and Stephany were both nice to me. But even
though they were wise to the ways of the street, one
night both of them got busted. I realized then how
much I appreciated the security I got from them when
I came back to the apartment. But now they were
gone, and I was all alone. That was frightening.

Life on the street was getting more difficult all the
time. Every so often I'd run into a pervert. A couple
of times I had to pull my switchblade—and that
stopped them.

But with Maria and Stephany gone, I was worried
about protection. Maybe I ought to get a pimp to take
care of me.

And yet I had heard such terrible stories about
those guys, and I'd seen some of their girls. If they
didn't go along with what the pimp said, they'd end up
with busted noses and black eyes! Whenever I saw one
of those girls standing on the street, all banged up, I

told myself that a pimp wasn't the answer for me. But I hated living alone; it did make me afraid.

It was Saturday night, and business was very good. I didn't know how much money I had made, but it was a lot. When I came back to the apartment, I really shot up. I don't remember how many bags I put in the needle, but I really got a high.

I must have fallen asleep on the couch, for the next thing I knew I was staring into the face of some unshaven, fierce-looking maniac.

Immediately I was wide awake and trembling with fear. "What do you want?" I demanded.

He smiled, but it quickly turned into a snarl. "I want you!" His voice dripped with evil.

"How did you get in here?" I yelled.

He reached into his pocket and held up a key. "I got in here with this. I mean, baby, it was no problem. And now I've got you right where I want you."

"Where did you get that key?" I demanded.

"That's none of your business. The only thing that matters is that I've got you to myself!"

He was frothing at the mouth; his clothes stank. It didn't take any great intelligence to size him up as a pervert.

Then he began to march around the room chanting a bunch of syllables I didn't understand. I sat there on the edge of the sofa watching him weave back and forth, and wondered what to do next. There was no telling what he planned to do to me. So I figured I'd better get rid of him right away. I reached into my bra for my trusty switchblade.

I couldn't feel it. I fumbled around; it wasn't there. I tried the other side. It wasn't there either. What had I—

The pervert let out a bloodcurdling scream. "And look what I have!" he yelled.

I jerked around and stared at him. He was waving something wildly around his head. My switchblade!

"How did you get that?" I demanded.

"Like I said, my little child, I know all about you girls. I know you carry switchblades, and I know where you carry them. Some of you even carry guns. But I'm smart. I mean, I have all the answers of the universe. I have been filled with the high power, and I have all wisdom. I'm out to judge the world!"

Not only a pervert, but a religious nut, too!

I jumped off the sofa and lunged at his fist. He anticipated that, and moved back, flicking open the switchblade. As I stepped forward, he kicked my feet out from under me, and I stumbled to the floor. I rolled over and stared up at him as he glared down at me. "My little flower child, don't you know I have power over you? I have claimed you, and you've been given to me. You are mine, and I have you now, and I shall use you in the way that you were destined to be used—as a sacrifice!" His hollow laughter echoed ominously through the room.

I scrambled to my feet and dashed over behind the sofa, where I watched him—terrified. He was going through all sorts of contortions. Now I knew what this pervert wanted. He didn't want my body for lust; he wanted it for some kind of a sacrifice!

On the street I had caught this kind of a nut looking at me. They stand around staring. When you walk by, you can feel their eyes burning holes through you. They're insane, but they're still walking the streets. This nut must be thinking he had to offer me as a sacrifice to some higher power to pay for his sins!

He dropped to his knees and began bowing to me, all the while keeping up that eerie chanting. But he still kept that opened switchblade in his hand.

I looked toward the door. Should I try to make a break for it? He watched my eyes, and then he moved over in front of the door. "No, no, little flower, do not think of fleeing. You are honored. You have been selected to die for a worthy cause. Your blood shall flow forth from this room and atone for my guilt."

"Now listen here, mister!" I screamed. "I don't know what you're up to, but I can tell you this right now. You try to kill me, and you're going to burn in the electric chair. I mean, mister, you're going to burn! So don't try anything!"

There was another bloodcurdling scream, and he lunged toward me. I ducked and ran the other way.

"Don't resist the power," he yelled, "or you will be struck by lightning and will turn into ashes!"

I figured that if I could circle far enough, I could make a break for the bathroom. If I could do that, at least I could lock the door and keep him out for a while. Maybe it would give me time to come up with a plan.

There was no way to reason with a nut like this. He was coming completely out of it. I knew other girls had faced perverts like this. The stories of girls being cut up and stuffed into garbage bags or pushed off tall buildings didn't hit the papers too often. But every so often we'd miss a girl from the street. And then the word got out: Some pervert had worked her over.

My heart beat wildly as I tried to weigh the options. The way he was guarding the door, I knew I couldn't get out. He would kill me here. The bathroom was my only hope.

Somehow I had to move him backwards. Maybe if I spoke to him romantically, that would do the trick.

So I moved a step toward him and in my most beguiling voice I said, "I know you're filled with love and power and glory and that you have all the wisdom of the universe. I'm sure you have the capacity for great love, and I so much desire to be loved. Please hold me close to soothe my wicked ways."

He stopped his chanting and stared, his eyes full of rage.

I took another step toward him.

"Don't you try to entice me, you filthy, good-for-nothing prostitute!" he screamed. "I've seen you take men off the street and bring them to the depths of hell. Don't you try to get near me!"

I smiled, took another step toward him and extended my arms. He stepped backward! It was working!

I took another step and calmly said, "Oh, no! You have it all wrong! I shall never do anything wrong with you, only that which is good and right."

"You dirty, filthy beast of the field!" he shouted. "You shall not entice me! Do you hear?"

I took a couple of quick steps. Somehow I had to keep him moving back, hoping that he wouldn't fly into a rage and lunge at me with that switchblade. With his strength, probably one lunge would kill me immediately. And I wasn't ready to die yet!

"Kiss me," I said as alluringly as I could.

Enraged, he ran from me, across the room. He rolled around on his feet, knife poised above his head, screaming, "Thou shalt not! Thou shalt not!"

I had him far enough from the door. But when I glanced toward the door to see if I could make it, he yelled, "Little flower, you put one hand on that door, and I shall sacrifice your hands immediately."

I sure didn't want that! I had to keep myself from even looking toward that door. And he never seemed to get far enough away from it for me to make a break.

For a moment I just stared at him. I wondered if he had ever killed anyone. Three weeks ago they found a girl in a deserted tenement on Forty-eighth Street. Her body had been badly burned. In fact, no one had yet identified her. No one in that neighborhood seemed to be missing, but I couldn't help wondering if this nut had lured her there and then sacrificed her. It sure seemed like it. And it sure seemed like he had me in mind for his next victim!

I had to keep cool. And one thing for sure: I was going to force myself to avoid looking at that door again.

Now if I could think of some way to get into that bathroom. He knew the apartment door was the only way out. And we were on the twelfth floor, so I sure couldn't jump from the bathroom window. Still, if I got away from him, I might have a chance.

Then I got an idea.

"Do you want to make a sweet-smelling sacrifice?" I asked.

He stared. Then he smiled. "Yes, flower child, your sacrifice shall be sweet, and it shall smell gloriously."

"Of course, my master," I responded. "Let me douse my body with fragrances from the far corners of the world. Then when I shall be offered, it shall indeed smell sweet."

A sinister smile covered his face. "Yes! Yes! That's wonderful! Be beautiful and sweet and full of fragrance!"

"I shall go and douse my body," I said, "and you shall be pleased."

"Yes! Yes! How wonderful!"

With that, I turned and walked slowly toward the bathroom. He didn't make a move.

Once inside the bathroom, I closed the door slowly and locked it. So far that act hadn't enraged him.

But what was I going to do now? I went over and threw open the bathroom window and stared down at the street. Not a soul around. I thought of yelling. But if he heard that, he would come busting through that door in no time, and I'd be offered right then and there. Help might be on the way, but not soon enough.

I had to think of something!

I glanced around the bathroom to see what I might use as a weapon. Maybe if I broke a bottle and lunged at him, I could kill him. But if I missed, that would be the end of me. I remembered how he had knocked my feet out from under me. He probably had studied karate.

My eyes noticed a book of matches. *Would he use those to start his burnt offering?* I wondered. Maybe I'd better flush them down the toilet.

That's when another idea struck me. I grabbed a towel, struck a match, and touched it to the end of the towel. When it was burning well, I placed it out the window.

It was a long chance. Would someone see it and call the fire department? Or maybe the smoke would rise and the people above me would call the fire department. If they came, maybe I could get out.

The towel was really burning now, I hoped it wouldn't set the whole building on fire. I slammed the end of the window over the edge of the towel. It was really burning, and the smoke was rising. Now if some-one—

My thoughts were interrupted by a banging on the bathroom door. "All right, flower child," the man screamed, "you've had enough time to douse your body with perfume. Come now and offer thyself."

I needed more time. "Yes, one more dousing," I responded, "and I'll be ready. This takes time. And you are going to be so happy with the sacrifice. It is going to smell so beautiful!"

I glanced at the bathroom window. Flames continued to shoot upward, and lots of smoke billowed. I kept hoping, and I even pleaded with God. I wasn't much for praying, but I'd never been in a jam like this one before. "God, please let someone see that fire; and, somehow, spare me."

But supposing no one saw it? And supposing the building caught fire—and it looked like maybe that was happening. Then I would be the cause of many people being killed—and I would die with them. Or supposing I lived. When they found out I had set the fire, they would send me away to prison for arson!

The flames seemed almost too high, and I was really scared now. Why had I done something so foolish? I grabbed another towel, soaked it, and opened the window to beat the flames out. But when I did, the flames shot inward, and I had to slam the window down to keep from being burned.

The man pounded on the door, screaming, "That's it! Open the door now! The time has come!"

I looked at the burning towel and offered another prayer, pleading with God to somehow get me out of this mess.

Then I heard a siren! What a wonderful sound! I

looked down through the smoking window and could see the trucks coming.

And in the midst of it all, was that persistent pounding on the door. "Get out here now!" he screamed. "The moment has arrived! I can even smell the smoke of the sacrifice!"

I had to stall him. If I could just put him off for another two or three minutes, the firemen would be on this floor banging on doors. Maybe if I shocked him —Yes, that was it. Maybe if he saw me unclothed, he would demand that I get dressed.

It was a big chance, but otherwise he would rip that door down. So I slipped off my clothes and opened the bathroom door. He stood there completely flabbergasted.

"No! No!" he screamed. "The sacrifice must not be made this way. This is terrible! This is evil! Flower child, no!"

"Please forgive me," I said as I bowed to him. "I thought this was the way you wanted me for the sacrifice."

The crazed man pulled the bathroom door shut with one hand and covered his eyes with the other. "I must not look upon such evil! Quick! Be clothed! Hurry! Already the smoke of the sacrifice begins to ascend to the higher power."

It worked! He wanted to be outside while I got dressed. I had gained some time. I pulled my clothes on and looked down through the smoke. The firemen were hooking up hoses and extending a huge ladder up in this direction.

Just then I heard men out in the hallway yelling, "Fire! Fire!" Would they stop at my door?

A loud explosion answered that question. They

must have blown the apartment door down. And I could hear the pervert yelling, "No! No! Get out of here, you evil men! I must have my sacrifice! I must have my sacrifice!"

I heard other men's voices, and one of them yelled, "He's crazy! He's crazy! Let's get him out of here!"

Hoping that now I was safe, I opened the bathroom door. Some firemen had subdued the pervert.

"Come here, quick!" I yelled. "This is where it's coming from!"

Three men ran toward me with fire extinguishers, and I pointed to the bathroom window. They brushed past me, threw open the window, and in minutes had the fire out. Part of the window frame had caught on fire, but they quickly had things under control.

"How in the world did that one start?" one of the firemen asked.

I was shaking so much and was so terrified by what I had been through, that instead of answering, I just broke down and started to sob. I pointed toward the crazy man on the floor. "He almost killed me! He almost killed me!"

A couple of policemen arrived about that time and took custody of the pervert. "Did he really try to kill you, ma'am?" they asked.

I nodded. "He's crazier than you could ever imagine," I said. "He wanted to offer me as a burnt sacrifice to some higher power."

"Young lady," the policeman said, "you don't know how lucky you are. We have been after someone who has been burning bodies. Maybe this is the guy. A couple of weeks ago we picked up a badly burned body, and we knew it was the work of someone who is crazy."

"You mean that girl over on West Forty-eighth?"
The officer nodded. "Yeah, she's the one. She had
a bunch of stab wounds. Evidently some loony had
built a fire to offer her as a sacrifice."

I shuddered as I said, "I'm sure this is the guy you're
looking for. He said he was going to offer me as a
sacrifice to atone for his sins."

Somehow the crazed man was able to wrestle free
and jump to his feet. He grabbed the switchblade from
a table and held it high. Everybody jumped back. Then
he glared at me and screamed, "Let me at her! I must
sacrifice! I must!"

He lunged toward me, and the two policemen
sprang into action with their clubs. Then it seemed
that everybody converged on the guy. The switchblade went sprawling across the floor, and all the men
—policemen and firemen—were caught up in making
sure he didn't get away again.

All I could think of was getting out of that place. I
wasn't in the mood to answer a lot of questions, so I
took a few quick steps and was out in the hallway. All
kinds of people were running around out there, so I
just got lost in the crowd heading down the stairs.

I really couldn't afford to answer their questions. If
they found out I was a prostitute and a junkie, they
might lock me up. I had a habit now—even I admitted
it to myself. If they locked me up, that would mean
kicking the habit cold turkey. I couldn't bear the
thought of that. If they searched my apartment and
found my works, I could be busted for that.

Down in the street great confusion reigned. People
kept pointing up at the apartment. I heard someone
say, "I think that has to be arson. A fire like that had

to have been deliberately set. What kind of nut would do something like that?"

I wanted to tell them I had to do it to save my own skin. But would they understand? Would I be charged with arson?

This place presented too many problems now, so I turned and walked down the street. Once again I had nowhere to go—and nothing but the clothes on my back. Well, it sure made me think about getting a pimp. I needed someone to protect me.

I found a pimp, but not until it was too late did I realize I had made a tragic mistake!

10 My legs felt like rubber as I walked aimlessly. I guess that experience with the pervert really knocked me for a loop. It isn't every night that a girl finds herself fighting for her life like that. I hoped against hope that something like that would never happen again. And yet somehow I knew it was almost inevitable. Maybe next time I wouldn't be so lucky.

I suddenly realized I had been walking down Eighth Avenue toward Forty-second Street. This was the bottom of the world. The area reeked with perverts, junkies, prostitutes, homosexuals, peep shows, and filthy porno shops.

At the corner of Forty-second and Eighth I spotted a coffee shop open. Maybe a cup of coffee would help calm me down. Getting off would help me more, but I'd settle for the coffee now. It would get me off these rubbery legs for a few minutes, and maybe I could figure out my next move.

Only a few people were in the coffee shop at that hour. I recognized them as junkies—like me. But I sure didn't feel like associating with them. I was too exhausted and depressed to make any kind of conversation, so I sat on a stool by myself.

I sat there drinking coffee, thinking, wondering, and trying to regain my composure. I was still shaky.

As I was drinking my third cup of coffee, a guy sat on the stool next to me. I glanced over. Wow! Was he good-looking! And dressed! He must have had something going for him.

"Hey, baby, what's happening?" he said breezily.

"Aw, nothing, nothing at all," I responded.

"I mean, baby, you look like you walked all the way from California. I saw you sitting here with your eyes half open. What's the matter? Haven't you slept for a week?"

Self-consciously I brushed back my hair from my face. "Oh," I said, "I didn't know I looked that bad. I just couldn't sleep, so I decided to come down for some coffee. Sorry I don't look beautiful to you."

He laughed as he said, "I mean, baby, I didn't mean to get personal or anything like that. Just trying to make conversation. I just couldn't help wondering what a good-looking chick like you was doing down here. Never seen you here before."

"Well, I just came into town the day before yesterday. I'm from Omaha, Nebraska, and I thought maybe I could make it on Broadway. I studied acting in college, and they told me this was the place to go. Either here or Hollywood. Hollywood doesn't seem to me to be as glamorous as the theater, so I headed for New York. But, man, it sure is hard getting a job here—

even though it seems like there's a theater on every corner."

"Now isn't that a coincidence!" the man replied. "I just happen to be an agent. I have fifteen people working for me. A lot of directors call me for my actresses, so I'm sure I could get you a job. In this business you got to have the right connections." He leaned over and whispered confidentially: "It's not *what* you know; it's *who* you know."

Now what had I gotten myself into? I'd led this guy on, and here I'd run into a dumb agent. How could I get him off my back?

Just then a police officer walked in and yelled, "Okay, everybody out! I mean you people standing over there!"

I whirled around. The cop stood in the doorway, billy club in hand. Then I looked over at the waitress. Why was a cop throwing everybody out?

"I said, everybody move!" he yelled again. "And I mean, move!"

I slid off my stool, but the guy next to me grabbed my arm. "Hold it," he said. "He's not talking about you."

We watched the junkies start moving out. The waitress came over and asked, "Fill up your coffee?"

"Hey, what's going on?" I asked.

"Aw, it's those junkies," she replied. "They don't really want coffee or anything like that. They just come in here to buy and sell drugs. I have to call the cops about five or six times a night. If the cops didn't come, we'd go out of business."

Soon the agent and I and the waitress were the only ones left in the coffee shop. "If I had my way about it," the agent said expansively, "I'd back up a police van to the door and load all those junkies in it and cart them off to jail. That's where they belong—in jail."

I wondered if the guy knew I was messed up too. Should I tell him?

"What are you doing after you finish your coffee?" he asked.

"Oh, I guess I'll go back to the apartment and get some sleep," I lied. "Then I'll look for a job again. You think you really could get me one?"

"Well, I can't guarantee that, baby. I haven't seen you act. But I'd sure love to try."

"That's mighty nice of you, mister. You look like . . ."

I never finished the sentence because just then there was a loud crack, and glass exploded everywhere. I turned around to see a brick that had been thrown through the plate glass window skid toward a stop just a few feet away from where we were sitting.

Who in the world would be throwing a brick at me? Or maybe they were throwing it at the agent? Some disgruntled client—

The waitress let out a round of curses that filled the air. She called those junkies every name she could think of. Apparently she had seen who threw the brick. She headed for the door yelling, "Police! Police!"

In a few moments the cop who had thrown everybody out was back inside.

"It was Frankie Peluso," the waitress screamed. "That dirty, stinking pill head! He doesn't know what he's doing most of the time. I have more trouble with him than with anyone."

"Frankie again, huh?" the officer repeated. "I guess I'll have to bust him for the fiftieth time. When that kid takes those pills, he doesn't know what's going on."

With that the cop took off, apparently looking for Frankie.

The waitress, obviously agitated and upset, came over and said, "I'm sorry, folks. but I'm going to have to close up. Those junkies are taking over this coffee shop. I'll just have to close the place until I can get that window fixed."

The agent paid for his coffee and mine, and we walked outside into the crowd that had gathered. That's one thing about the city. No matter what the hour of the day or night, any excitement seems to draw an immediate crowd.

As we stood there, the agent said, "By the way, my name is Harding Mason. What's yours?"

"Debbie Carter."

"I guess, Debbie, we had a close call on that one, didn't we? Apparently old Frankie was upset because he had to leave the coffee shop and we didn't."

"Maybe he wasn't aiming at us," I responded. "When those young junkies get irritable, they just seem to go berserk."

"Listen, Debbie," Harding said, "why don't you come over to my apartment? We can talk a little bit more there. I need to get some information about your background and experience and where you've tried to get jobs. You never know, baby; this could lead to the launching of a great career! I've helped a few girls."

I studied Harding. Could I trust him? I sure couldn't invite him to my apartment. I didn't dare go back there. So if I went to his, maybe that would throw him off on that approach. And I really didn't have anywhere to go.

"Sounds like a good idea!" I responded. "I appreciate your inviting me over."

We walked along Broadway, and Harding pointed out some of the shows that were playing. I kept trying to think of what I could tell him about my supposedly being an actress. I'd never gone to a play in a theater in my life. And if he kept probing, it wouldn't be long before he would find out I had lied. But so what? I'd think of another lie. Besides, I felt a little safer around him, and a handsome brute like this didn't come along every day!

At Forty-sixth Street we turned and walked to the middle of the block and entered a run-down apartment house.

This seemed strange. I thought agents made good money—especially if he was the agent for a number of girls. These guys collect ten percent of their clients' earnings, and some actresses made awfully good money. But this apartment certainly looked like a sleazy old place.

Evidently Harding was reading my thoughts. "I know this isn't the greatest place," he said apologetically. "But, you see, I'm really trying to save money because I want to do my own Broadway play. If you get successful, you can become a millionaire overnight! I used to stay on the East Side in a very expensive apartment overlooking the river, but I wasn't able to save much money. So I moved down here. I'm close to the business down here too."

I just nodded. If he wanted to put up with a mess like this to save money, that was his business.

I stopped at the elevator. "Uh, it's not working anymore," Harding said. "We'll have to walk up."

This place really was a dump. The stairs smelled

terrible; someone had used them as a bathroom! Parts of the walls had been ripped out.

We got to the third floor, and Harding unlocked his apartment and flicked on the one light in the place. He motioned me in, and he followed.

The click of the lock behind us sounded so ominous. No one on earth had any idea where I was. Why had I been so stupid as to agree to come here? Wasn't one pervert a night enough?

I glanced around at the depressing mess. No windows. And one room only. At one side was a double bed. On the opposite end were a sink and refrigerator and stove. On the adjoining wall was a closet door with four locks on the outside. That looked strange—almost like a bank vault. It made me even more nervous.

Harding must have sensed my uneasiness. "Don't be afraid, Debbie. I know it isn't much of a place, but I get it for seventy-five dollars a month. You sure can't beat that price."

In the middle of the room he had a small table and two chairs. I pulled out a chair and sat down.

Harding walked over and put his hands on the back of the chair. "Want to get off?" he asked.

I looked up at him. What did he know about drugs? He certainly didn't seem like a junkie.

I decided to stay cool. "Do I want to do what?" I repeated.

"You know, get high. Baby, I've got the best heroin in town, and you look like you need a fix about now."

As soon as he mentioned heroin, something clicked. Maybe this was his way of getting actresses to work for him. Well, he didn't have to tempt me with drugs. I was ready for a fix.

"You certainly don't look like a junkie," I said. "How come you're offering me drugs?"

"Oh, I don't know. I thought maybe you would like to try it. You look like you need something to perk you up."

"Now, Harding, you're not a pusher, are you? I mean, like you're trying to get me to take some drugs and get me hooked and then start to supply my habit? You're not one of those guys, are you?"

"No way, baby, am I going to try to sell drugs. In this state you can get life for that."

"Yeah, I know," I said. "It's real bad news, real bad."

Steve DiSilva was probably in the slammer doing life for his cocaine dealings. Oh, I was lucky I didn't get busted with him. Somebody must be watching out for me!

"Okay, Harding, you're on. Sure, I'd like to get high."

He pulled up a chair next to me, raised one leg, and slipped off his shoe. Then he knocked the heel slightly. It came off in his hand, and inside it were three bags of heroin.

"My goodness!" I said in surprise. "I've never seen anything like that before. How did you ever think of it?"

"A friend of mine is in the shoe-repair business. He also sells dope. Actually, his shoe-repair business is just a front, and the guy's got tons of money. He's the one who came up with this idea. When cops frisk you on the street, they never look at the heels of your shoes."

Harding set the heroin on the table. "Come here, and let me show you something else," he said.

We walked across the room to a little partition. Behind it was the toilet. As he reached into the toilet bowl, he said, "Down in here is where I keep my works." He fumbled around in the water and came up with a small metal case. Inside was a set of works.

"You see," he explained, "if the cops bust in, they look for your works. I got another friend in the plumbing business, and he built this special compartment. Cops will check your toilet, but, believe me, they won't reach down into the water. Cops may be tough, but they're still too squeamish to mess around with stinking water."

I could feel my stomach turning over.

"I know it's not very pleasant, Debbie," he said. "But I also know that if you get busted for having works, you're going to do time. So I'd rather leave dirty water in the toilet and stop a cop, than let them find my works. Besides, this little case is completely watertight. Nothing can get in there."

That made me feel a little better.

We walked over to the kitchen sink, and Harding quickly made the fix and handed me the needle. "Want to drill yourself?"

"Yeah. Let me use your belt."

I wrapped the belt around the muscle in my arm, pumped up my veins, and drilled myself in the armpit. Harding stood there watching.

I used the whole needle and released the belt. Then it happened. Harding had good stuff. I mean, good stuff.

The high took away my worries of what had happened and what might happen. All I could see was Harding standing there. He was the answer to my dreams.

I waited and waited for him to get off, but he just stood there. "Hey, man," I said, "that's good stuff. Aren't you going to get off with me?"

He simply shook his head. "In my business you never want to use this stuff," he said.

That should have warned me, but I was so out of things by then that I really didn't care.

The rest of the morning I sat around nodding. About eleven Harding let me get off again. I've never felt so good in all my life! In fact, that day I got off four times. All free!

About ten that evening Harding and I were lying on the bed, when he got up and announced, "It's time to go to work."

I blinked in wonder. Agents didn't work at this time of night, did they?

"What's the matter with you?" I asked. "You work swing shift or something? I thought agents worked during the day."

Harding grabbed me and pulled me off the bed. What in the world was happening? Why would he do something like that?

"Debbie, when I say we got to go to work, I mean you."

"Oh, Harding," I said, "I've got to level with you. I've never had any experience as an actress in my life. Everything I told you this morning was a big lie. I'm not really from Nebraska. To tell you the honest truth, you've latched onto a prostitute who is hooked on drugs. I'm sorry for misleading you. I ought to pay you for the drugs, but I've got to get up and go."

Then I saw his open hand moving toward my face. Slap! Oh, it stung! I jumped back.

"Listen, Harding, don't be so belligerent. So I lied. I told you I'd pay you for the drugs. So sue me."

He grabbed me by the shoulders and shook me. "Let me make it as plain as I can, Debbie. I want you to get out there on that street and hustle. You're working for me now!"

Oh, no! Harding was no agent; he was a pimp!

"Listen," I screamed, "there is absolutely no way I'm going to go out there and hustle for some pimp!"

I should have backed away before I said that. He held onto my shoulder with one hand. With the other he slapped my face repeatedly until I was beginning to feel the blood come.

I reached inside my bra for my switchblade. I'd forgotten! That pervert had taken it. By now the cops had it.

I was defenseless. I pulled away and tried to cover my face and protect myself, but it seemed useless. I was in the clutches of a vicious pimp.

I didn't know how I was going to get out of this mess, but I told myself that no way was I ever going to hustle for this maniac.

He grabbed me again and threw me up against the wall. Then he grabbed a coat hanger from the steel rod nearby and whipped my backside mercilessly. He kept beating and beating, and I kept screaming and screaming.

"What did you say, Debbie?" he yelled. "What did you say? Well, I say you're going out there on that street and hustle for me. You hear me?"

I kept screaming that I never would do it.

The pain from the continued beating with the coat hanger was excruciating. It felt as though those blows

that hit across my hips drew blood. I thought I was
going to die.

After what seemed like an eternity of his beating me,
I meekly said, "Okay, Harding, have it your way. I give
up."

He didn't answer. Instead he dragged me over to
that padlocked closet door. By this time I was on the
floor at his feet, and he put one foot on my head. "One
move out of you," he screamed, "and I'll smash every
bone in your pretty little head!"

I was no match for his brute strength, so I lay there
very quietly as he unlocked all four locks. Then he
opened the door ever so slightly and threw me into
that room. I quickly glanced around and couldn't see
a thing in the room. Then he slammed the door, and
I was in total darkness.

"You stay in there and think about it for a while,
baby," Harding yelled. "If you're good, I may let you
out, or I may never let you out!"

I heard all four locks click, and I pushed against the
door. It didn't even budge! No way was I going to get
out of this one. He had made me his prisoner.

I fell to my knees and started to sob. What had I
gotten myself into this time? I'd become a slave to a
maniac. I'd heard about vicious pimps. If you tried to
escape, they'd kill you—I mean, literally.

My wounds stung so bad I could hardly move. I sure
couldn't sit down. But as I knelt there, sobbing and
aching, I felt something brush against my leg. I
reached down and felt my hand plunge into the side
of a furry body. A rat! As he skidded across the floor
from my blow, he began to hiss loudly. I jumped up
and screamed, "Harding! Harding! Please let me out!
There's a rat in here! Please! Please! I'm terrified!"

He laughed like a maniac and yelled back, "Don't worry about a little rat, Debbie. I have six rats in there, and they are hungry."

My heart beat wildly. Those rats probably smelled blood. In a few moments they would savagely attack me and kill me. Oh, what a horrible way to die!

I pounded and pounded on the door screaming, "Harding! Let me out! Please let me out! Whatever you say, I'll do it! I promise! I promise! I promise!"

My hysterical promises were met only with more of that raucous laughter. I'd escaped from one maniac only to be taken prisoner by another!

I felt a rat brush my feet. I tried to climb the walls, screaming all the while.

"Debbie, I'll see you later," Harding called. "I need to go out and get a cup of coffee. I can't stand all the noise in this apartment."

He couldn't do this to me! One human being had no right to subject another human being to torture like this. Any minute now those rats would begin gnawing at my flesh. I was no match for six angry, hungry rats!

In terror I screamed again, "Harding! Harding! Please listen to me! Whatever you say, you can have. I mean, right now put me out on the streets, and I'll do whatever you say. Please! Please!"

I waited. No answer. Had he already gone?

Then I heard the door rattle, and one by one the locks clicked. Just as soon as the door opened, he pulled me outside and slammed the door behind me.

"Don't want those rats to escape," he said. "They are vicious."

I stared at him openmouthed. My heart raced wildly. I was absolutely more terrified than I have ever been before. And he just stood there like it was an everyday

occurrence! I couldn't believe that anyone would subject another human being to the kind of terror he had
put me through in an attempt to break my will.

"Harding, whatever you say, whatever you say," I
kept repeating.

He grabbed me by my blouse and pulled me up
where he was looking me straight in the face. "Now
listen, Debbie, let's get a few things straight. You be
a nice little girl, and I'll take care of you. But you be
a bad girl, and you know what will happen to you. I'm
going to put you back in that room. Those rats are
always hungry. So if you don't do exactly what I say,
you'll end up as rat food. And let me tell you, they're
vicious. And poisonous!"

Hysterically I screamed, "Harding, don't ever do
that to me again! I promise that whatever you say
goes. What you say goes!"

Harding smiled triumphantly. "Well, that's better.
Okay, baby, get out on the street and bring big daddy
home some money."

"You mean you want me out on the street looking
like this?" I asked.

"Listen, kid," he responded, "there are guys out
there who will pay for anything. Whether you're
bruised, bleeding, or whatever. Somebody's going to
pick you up because they feel sorry for you."

With that he pushed me toward the door and followed me down the three flights of stairs to the street.
Every step was pain.

We headed for Forty-second Street—the worst
place in the city to prostitute. That was where all the
perverts hung out.

As we walked along, Harding said, "Debbie, I knew
who you were the moment I saw you in that coffee

shop. I saw the tracks on your arm. I didn't believe your story. But it really doesn't matter because now, baby, you are working for me. You hear?''

I nodded. No way in the world was I going to do anything to cross up Harding again. Rats scared me to death, and I knew Harding was maniac enough to throw me in there again. And next time he probably wouldn't let me out so quickly!

So I stood on the corner of Forty-second and Eighth. Harding stood across the street watching me. And it hit me that I had wanted a pimp for protection. Well, I had protection. But in the process I had become a slave to a pimp. First a prostitute; then a junkie; now a slave.

I wondered how long I was going to be able to survive in this jungle. In my foggy mind I knew that most girls didn't last long when they got to this stage.

Debbie Carter—the runaway who was going to be different. Ha! I'd be better off dead. But suppose I did die. What then?

11 The life of a drug addict is bad enough. So is the life of a prostitute. But when you combine the two, it makes the worst in the world.

Sometimes the drug you bought was nothing—just milk sugar. Sometimes the johns would try to kill you.

But one thing about Harding—he always did stay close by. Of course, his reasons for keeping me alive were strictly selfish. He wanted the money I brought in.

There was such bitter jealousy among the pimps.

Every so often I had the chance to work for someone else. But whenever another pimp would talk to me, Harding would threaten to kill me if I tried to double-cross him. Or worse yet—put me back in that closet with those rats! I shuddered in terror at the thought.

I wanted so desperately to break away from Harding. And yet I knew if I tried it, that would be the end of me. I learned that on the streets he had the reputation of being very mean. I was caught in his web. The more I tried to get loose, the worse it got. And the beatings kept up.

As the bleary days trailed into weeks and months, I despaired of any hope. I needed more and more heroin to keep me going. Frequently I started getting sick and couldn't get high. I just shot the dope to take away the sickness. Every time I stuck that needle in my arm, I hated myself. And every time I looked at Harding, I wanted to kill him. And then to kill myself.

One evening I was so tired and sick that I thought I would go home a little early. Harding wasn't around, at least not where I could see him. Maybe he'd never know.

But when I opened the apartment door, Harding was sitting there. As soon as he saw me, he flew into a rage. I tried to back out, but he grabbed me by the hair and threw me to the floor. He punched me and started whipping me with a coat hanger.

As I screamed, he yelled, "Listen, Debbie, it's not time to come in yet! Go back out there on the street!"

"Harding," I pleaded, "please don't beat me. I'm so tired and so sick that I just wanted to come home a little bit early, that's all."

"Listen, baby, you come home when I tell you it's

time to come home—and not a minute before. Now get back out there!"

He jerked me up by my hair. "How much money have you made so far?" he demanded.

I knew if I told him how little it was, he would go into another rage and beat me some more. So I lied. "I made five hundred dollars."

He softened. "Well, that's more like it," he said. "Okay, give it to me, and get back out there."

I reached into my bra and handed him the fifty dollars I knew was there.

He counted it out and screamed, "Listen, Debbie, are you holding out on me? There's only fifty dollars here! You owe me four hundred fifty dollars!"

Now I really was in a jam. This called for another lie. "Harding, I did make five hundred dollars, but I got ripped off by another pimp."

At my mention of the word *pimp*, Harding flew into another rage. "Who was the creep?" he demanded.

"George Turner."

George Turner was another vicious pimp. He and Harding were known as the worst. And they hated each other passionately.

"That dirty, good-for-nothing George!" Harding screamed. "I know, Debbie, that he's been trying to get you into his stable. But this is absolutely the lowest, for him to rip you off. How did it happen?"

I had to think of something quick.

"Well, I guess you could call it ripping me off. But this is what he told me. I went out with this guy. As soon as I got back on the street, George asked me what I did with the guy, so I told him. Now, I've never seen the guy before, but he paid real well. I mean, the guy paid me four hundred dollars. So I kind of bragged and told George the guy was a big spender. George asked how much money he had paid me. When I said, 'four hundred dollars,' George slapped me across the face and said, 'Don't you know that man belongs to me?' And so I said, 'What do you mean by that?' And George said that was one of his girls' johns and I had no business coming into his territory."

"What's this? What's this?" Harding interrupted. "I don't know nothing about no territories for johns. All I know is who I own and who George owns. Why that stinking rat! He's got his nerve trying to set up territories."

"Well, that's what I thought," I said. "But before I knew what was happening, he jerked open my blouse and snatched the money. I'm standing there screaming, and George just turned and walked down the street laughing."

Harding was red with rage. "That's it," he said. "That is it! I've had enough of that guy!" He walked to a drawer and pulled out a .45 pistol. "We'll see about territories." Then he said to me, "You get back out on that street. And you better get four hundred fifty dollars real quick. You still owe that to me."

I started to protest, but he slapped me across the face. "Listen to what I'm telling you!" he screamed. "Get out there and raise four hundred fifty dollars, or I'll put you in with those rats! You understand what I mean?"

He pushed me to the door and followed me to the street, snarling at me all the way.

What was I going to do now? If George was around, there was going to be a big shoot-out. Harding would believe me before he would believe George, even if George denied ripping me off.

We got down to Forty-second Street, and Harding started inquiring about where George was. Someone said he had gone over to Times Square. As Harding stomped off in that direction, he yelled at me, "Okay, Debbie, I'll be back in a few minutes. You better get busy, or you know what's going to happen to you!"

I watched Harding head toward Broadway. Would he find George and kill him?

And what was I going to do? How could I make four hundred fifty dollars? I knew one thing for sure: I had better start turning a trick! If I did get enough money, Harding would calm down.

But what would happen if George convinced Harding that I had lied? Now what kind of a mess was I in?

I walked back and forth, trying to attract the attention of some johns, but no one seemed to pay any heed.

Then two cops headed in my direction. I turned and moved the other way. They kept following. I turned the corner, walked halfway up the block, and stood in a doorway. The cops kept heading toward me.

I crossed the street and turned and watched. Would they still tail me? No. This time they kept walking straight ahead.

I drew a deep breath of relief. All I needed now was to get busted. Then again, maybe it wouldn't be so bad. Sure, I'd have to spend time in jail. But at least Harding couldn't kill me there. And I'd be safe from his rats!

I went back to the block and kept working. But still nobody. Then out of nowhere this middle-aged woman walked up to me and said, "Did you know that Jesus loves you?"

I jumped back in surprise. She was well dressed and

seemed to be in her mid-forties. A younger girl accompanied her; she looked to be in her mid-twenties. I just stood there looking at them blankly.

The lady smiled and repeated, "Did you know that Jesus loves you?" Then she added, "And I love you too."

Oh, no! A religious fanatic! I sure didn't have the time to spend with one of these nuts. I had to get working and make four hundred fifty dollars, so I had to get rid of her.

"Listen, lady," I responded, "I don't know about Jesus loving me. But I can tell you one thing for sure: You don't love me!"

She just smiled sweetly and said, "Oh, but I do! In fact, I love many, many girls just like you."

She must be one of the persistent ones. They could take a good chunk out of a night!

"Now listen here, lady," I said indignantly, "I don't know you, and you don't know me. Here I am standing out on the street, minding my own business, and you walk up and tell me you love me. I mean, no way, lady, can anybody make a statement like that. You don't know a thing about me. Besides, there's not that kind of love in this world."

I kept spouting off like that, but before I knew it, she threw her arms around me and hugged me.

That caught me so much off guard that I didn't know what to do. So I just stood there. And then she began to pat my back and whispered, "Yes, I really do love you."

Strange sensations started going over me, and vaguely, like a voice from the distant past, I could feel an old judge hugging me in his chambers and telling me he loved me. Could it be—?

The lady gently took her arm down and smiled so tenderly. I'll never forget that smile and that hug as long as I live. There was something radiant about her. I'd never seen anything like it before in a person's face. How could she walk up and tell me that Jesus loved me and she loved me too?

"I'm Mrs. Benton from the Walter Hoving Home," the lady said. "And this is Randy Aquafredda."

I nodded toward Randy.

"And what is your name?" Mrs. Benton asked.

The way she asked it and the way she smiled made it so hard to resist. What difference did it make if she knew my name? So I blurted out, "Debbie Carter."

"Oh, that's a nice name. In fact, we've got several Debbies at our home, and they're all such sweet girls. I'm sure you're just as sweet as they are."

If she only knew!

I couldn't help but wonder what on earth she was talking about. What kind of home would have more than one Debbie? But more than that, why in the world would she walk up to me and tell me that she loved me? It must be some kind of a new game. "Randy and I, along with my husband and some other members of the staff, are out here on Forty-second Street tonight telling girls like you that Christ has beautiful plans for their lives," Mrs. Benton explained. "And those plans aren't to be drug addicts here in the street."

Did she know about me? I thought I'd better lie. It might be some kind of a trap. "Oh, yes, these drug addicts really need help," I said. "I mean, they're very bad people. You see, I'm just a secretary and am waiting for my boyfriend to come along. He should be here any minute now."

The two of them laughed, and that unnerved me. "Now, Debbie," Mrs. Benton said, "you don't need to be afraid of us. We're not the police or anything like that. We know you need help. We know all about you."

"Know all about me?" I repeated in amazement. Were they social workers who had finally traced me here?

"Well, maybe not all," Randy admitted. "We don't know where you live or things like that. But we do know that you're out here doing things to support your habit."

I stared at her. Then she about blew me away when she said, "And Debbie, I know what you're going through. I was once a junkie."

"You were?" I asked. "Then what in the world are you doing back in this area?"

She just smiled. "The agony and terror that you're going through is something I've also experienced," she said. "But now all that's been changed. Jesus came into my heart, and I've been really born again. Now I'm experiencing the plans God has for my life, and it's so exciting!"

"I went to Randy when she was in jail and told her about Jesus," Mrs. Benton said. "Then she came to our home. She spent a year with us and graduated, and for many years now she has been free from her life as a drug addict. Randy is such a wonderful Christian girl, and she likes to share with girls like you what Christ can do for them. My husband and I have this home upstate in Garrison. It's filled with girls who are reaching out for help. And, thank God, they are being helped."

"Now wait a minute," I interruped. "Let's go

through this again. You say you have a home for girls, upstate, and that you're coming down here to tell girls like me about Jesus. Are you for real?"

They both laughed again. "Honestly, we're for real," Mrs. Benton responded. Then she opened her purse and pulled out a brochure showing the Walter Hoving Home. It looked like such a beautiful, peaceful place. She explained to me something about the Lord giving them this lovely thirty-seven-acre estate in Garrison with a large, three-story mansion on it. They had started a school where girls were taught to live according to the teachings of the Bible. She told me the Bible taught us how to really live and to enjoy the things that God wanted to give us. They had a couple of horses, she said, and a stream ran through the estate, and there was a large swimming pool. She said they all had such a wonderful time together.

As I looked at those pictures of the home, it seemed so inviting. Nostalgically it reminded me of those good years with the Greens. But somehow I felt what Mrs. Benton was talking about just wasn't for me.

Randy must have sensed my doubts. "You know, Debbie," she said, "you probably don't believe what we're telling you. Maybe this all seems too good to be true. But I know it is true.

"A few years ago I moved to Greenwich Village. There I was introduced to speed, LSD, and finally heroin. I didn't realize at the time that this would lead to seven long years of addiction, several jail sentences, and a complete moral breakdown."

She brushed a tear from her eye and went on. "And, Debbie, it wasn't that I didn't want to try to help myself. I really did. I wanted out but couldn't get out. I tried methadone, hospitals, and therapy, but there didn't seem to be any help for me. I could be put away physically, but then I discovered I was still hooked mentally. I was no longer the free person I had fought to become. Instead, I was bound in guilt and hate."

I stood there staring at her. "Really?" I asked. "You really were a junkie?"

"I really was," she answered. "And I tell you, Debbie, things sure got bad. This girl friend of mine and I got off together, and right in my arms she died of an overdose. I just couldn't stand it. She was such a wonderful friend of mine, and I was so ridden with guilt because of her death. In fact, as I looked at her body, I wished over and over that it had been me. I secretly hoped I would overdose too. From that day on I began taking too many barbiturates. I even had to write illegal prescriptions to get them."

No question about it; Randy was for real. She knew all the language. I'm sure she knew the hurt and the hate.

"Then I was arrested for the last time," Randy continued. "This time it was prison. The courts had seen me enough. While I sat in prison, I realized what a complete mess I had made of my life. In that dingy, filthy prison cell, I read a book called *Carmen* that someone had given me."

"My husband wrote that book," Mrs. Benton interrupted. "God has used it to help many girls."

"*Carmen* is a story about a girl drug addict who came to know Jesus and is now happy and free," Randy told me. "And Debbie, as I sat there in that cell, I wondered, *Could something like that happen to me?*"

This was so unreal! I was still aching from the beating Harding had given me. At this very moment Harding might be encountering George, and a bloody fight would take place. And at a time like this—to run into Mrs. Benton and Randy. This Mrs. Benton looked like a kindly mother. And Randy was just too much—radiant and so different. And for a moment I wondered, as she had, *Could this happen to me?*

There was no way that I deserved a break. I really deserved to be dead. But deep down inside I somehow believed there was a better way of life. If I stayed a junkie, I knew I would end up dead—either from an overdose or else Harding would kill me.

I turned to walk away, but Randy reached out and grabbed my arm. "Debbie," she said, "that's not the end of the story. I did more than wonder. I wrote to the address at the back of the book, and Mrs. Benton —the lady standing right here—was the one who came to the prison to visit me. I didn't think anything good could come out of her visit, but something beautiful did happen! Right in prison I asked Jesus Christ to come into my life and to replace all that I had destroyed. It was the most beautiful experience I've ever had. From that point on my life began to change for the better."

Mrs. Benton said, "Debbie, that's why we're here— to tell you the same thing that I told Randy. Jesus wants to come into your heart and change it all around."

I looked down at the pavement. Was I dreaming? Was there really hope? Here I was trapped and was worse off than a slave. I was continually being beaten, mutilated, and humiliated. I was worse off than the garbage on the street. There couldn't be any hope for someone as low-down as me.

I slowly shook my head. "It all sounds very nice," I said sadly, "but I guess it isn't for me."

Mrs. Benton put her arm around me and hugged me again. Then she whispered, "Debbie, I realize you probably can't trust anybody now. But let me assure you that what we're talking about is real. I believe Jesus brought us here especially to talk to you tonight. He wants to reach into your heart and do something good for you. All that hate, bitterness, resentment, discouragement, and all your hurts—He wants to take them out and put in His love. It's beautiful!"

I tried not to cry, but big tears splashed down my cheeks. When I looked over at Mrs. Benton, I saw she was crying too. I'd never met a woman like this in all my life. She *was* for real. Randy was crying too.

"Debbie, please give Jesus a chance," Mrs. Benton said. "You can be saved; it's so simple. Jesus died on the cross for your sins. And He arose from the dead so you could live forever. And right now He wants to pour into your life more love than you can possibly believe. He wants to heal all those scars and give you peace and joy and freedom—all the things you've always been searching for and have never found in this kind of life."

"And," Randy added, "we'd like to take you right now to the home up in Garrison. Right off the street. You can come with us now!"

That was a strange twist. I expected there would be a long waiting list and a lot of delays for something as great as that home sounded. Maybe even, they'd tell me that they'd like to help me but there just wasn't room.

"You mean right now?" I asked in amazement. "Just as I am?"

Mrs. Benton smiled. "Just as you are."

Was this the way out I had been searching for? If I

left with these people right now, I could get away from Harding's clutches.

Harding! No sooner had I thought about getting away from him than I saw him walking toward us. The way he was stomping, I knew he was still in a rage. I edged closer to Mrs. Benton and Randy.

When Harding spotted me, he yelled, "Debbie, come over here!"

Mrs. Benton and Randy looked his direction. Did they suspect he was my pimp? They seemed wise in the ways of the street.

"I said come here, Debbie!" Harding screamed again.

I didn't move. Did he find out that the whole story about George was a big lie? If I walked over there, would he start slapping me around? Besides, I felt safe standing here by Mrs. Benton and Randy.

When Harding saw I wasn't going to move, he walked over and grabbed my arm. "Listen, Debbie, I haven't found George yet. But you'd better be telling the truth! If that's another of your lies, it's all over for you, baby!"

He dug his fingers into my upper arm and squeezed. "You better bring in a thousand bucks tonight, or you're really going to get it. Now quit gabbing and get to work!"

Then he stomped off, yelling back, "I'll see you later after I take care of George."

"That your pimp?" Randy asked confidentially.

I nodded blankly.

"He looks like a mean one," Randy offered.

"You don't know the half of it, Randy. He's the most vicious guy on the street. I'm no better than a slave."

"Yeah, I've been there too," Randy sympathized.

"And let me tell you, Debbie, it doesn't get any better. There is absolutely no way out with that kind of a pimp. I don't want to scare you or anything, but looking at that character, I think it's about all over for you!"

Randy was so right. I knew Harding either was going to kill me, or he was going to push me so hard that I would kill myself. Especially after tonight when he caught up with George and found out I had told a pack of lies. Then it was going to be all over. With Harding in that kind of a rage, I was sure he would shoot me or put me in with those rats and let them gnaw me to death. That was more in keeping with his perverted nature.

"Debbie," Mrs. Benton said, "I don't know why, but I feel that I should insist that you come with us right now. We will take you in our van right up to the home tonight. We can hide you there; nobody will know where you are. But most important, there we can talk to you more about what it means to receive Jesus as your Saviour. I believe that you will experience a new life. The beautiful thing that God has done for Randy, He wants to do for you too. Why don't you give it a try? Please?"

"I really want to," I responded, "but you don't understand my problem. If my pimp doesn't see me later on, he's out to kill. And I mean kill."

Mrs. Benton just smiled that same sweet smile. "One of the first lessons you learn as a Christian is to trust the Lord," she said. "The Bible says that underneath us are the everlasting arms of God. That means that He's the one who is going to support us; He's the one who is going to protect us; He's the one who is going to help us. And He's the one who is going to take care of your pimp. Just turn him over to the Lord. What I'm saying is this: As you surrender your life to the Lord, He's going to be responsible for looking out for you. Wouldn't it be great to have God watching over you?"

All that sounded too good to be true; but I knew I had to find out. And I knew I might never have an opportunity like this again. "Yes," I said, after a moment's hesitation, "I think I will go with you. But we've got to get out of here right now. Harding will be back any minute. And he's packing a loaded .45 under his belt. And he'll use it!"

I didn't have to say anything else. Randy grabbed my arm and rushed me down the street toward their van. On the way we met the other people from the home, and Mrs. Benton quickly introduced them to me—including Reverend Benton, her husband, the director of the home. They all seemed to be so happy. Already I felt that I had made the right decision.

When they learned of my situation, we all quickly loaded into the van and headed upstate to Garrison.

Each mile we drove I breathed a little easier. It seemed so good to be getting out of the city again. Gradually hope was returning to my befuddled brain.

The girls just bubbled over with enthusiasm and love. They could hardly wait to take turns telling me their stories—some of them a lot like mine. Some had taken overdoses. Some had been into prostitution, alcoholism, drugs—all sorts of problems. But their stories all had a similarity—they learned that Jesus could make a difference in their lives, and they had been born again and their lives drastically changed.

They chattered on, telling me about what it was like at the home. They explained that they called Mrs.

Benton, Mom B. and Reverend Benton, to them, was
Brother B.

As I sat there listening, I just couldn't take it all in.
I felt as though I were riding with a van load of angels.
The miracles these girls told me about were absolutely
remarkable!

About an hour and a half after we left the city, we
drove onto the grounds of the Walter Hoving Home.
Through the moonlight I could see the beautiful trees
and landscape. Light flickered from the pool. It
seemed like heaven!

12 That night I slept like a baby. It was so good

being away from the city. But when I awakened, I knew
that kind of rest wouldn't last long. I still had to kick
my heroin habit, and it had to be cold turkey. I shuddered as I thought of the torment.

The second night I started feeling sick and so very
tense. My body cried out for the drugs I had been
giving it so regularly, and for which it had developed
a dependence.

The staff at the home sympathized with me and put
me in a room by myself. Some of them stayed and
prayed with me.

About midnight I was tossing in absolute agony.
One of the staff members, Linda Wahl, came in. She
smiled at me so sweetly. Then she said, "Debbie, I
know you're about to go through a severe testing. But
the best way to go through it is to start with Jesus."

I looked at her in wonder. Was she serious? Would
Jesus help me kick drugs?

"Linda," I responded, "whatever you think I should do, I'm ready. I'm sick to death of my old life. And I'm ready for whatever Jesus has for me in the future. I don't know if I can live through this kicking of the habit, but I'm sure going to try!"

"Hey, that's what I like to hear," Linda responded, wiping my forehead with her cool hand.

"There are many wonderful things you're going to learn as a Christian," she went on. "One of those is to learn to trust God. As you go through this kicking, He wants to go through it with you. And He will give you strength to endure it."

"Well, I certainly hope so," I answered weakly.

Linda smiled again. "Not hope so; we *know* so!"

In spite of how miserable I felt, I forced a smile. Linda certainly seemed to believe what she said. Besides, how could anyone refuse a beautiful smile like hers?

"The first thing you need to do, Debbie, is to receive Jesus as your personal Saviour," Linda told me. "Now I don't know if you're really going to understand this completely, but at least I'm going to share it with you. Receiving Jesus is very simple. People sometimes make it difficult. If they only knew how much Jesus wanted to come into their lives and change them."

"You mean to tell me that Jesus really wants to come into my life?" I asked. "Don't you know how sinful I've been? I mean, I've hit bottom! I've done terrible things to support my drug habit. I can't believe Jesus would want anyone like me."

She smiled that infectious smile again. "That's just it, Debbie. Though you may be dirty and filthy—absolutely the worst sinner on the face of the earth, Jesus died for you. In fact, if you were the only person on the earth and were absolutely the worst sinner who had ever lived, Jesus would still have died just for you! He died so you could be forgiven of your sins and enter a new life."

Now that was hard to believe. Would Jesus have died just for me? Here I was lost, lonely, without any friends, and absolutely worthless. Would He really die just for me?

"But," I protested, "you don't know me. And you remind me a lot of Mom B. When I stood on the street last night, do you know she just walked up to me and threw her arms around me and said she loved me? I mean, that was weird!"

Linda threw back her head and laughed. "Debbie, you'll get used to Mom B. She just loves everybody. I mean, you could be stinking like garbage that's been sitting around for two years, and she wouldn't care. She'd still throw her arms around you and hug you."

"Well, I was stinking! And I'll never forget her love for me."

Linda got serious. "Do you know why Mom B. can love someone like you, even when she doesn't know you?" she asked.

Without waiting for me to answer, she went on: "It's because she knows Jesus, and she lets the love of Jesus flow through her life. You see, it's the reality of Christ in her life that reaches out to touch someone like you. Believe me, it's for real."

I didn't doubt that!

"And, Debbie," Linda continued, "this is exactly what we're talking about. As you receive Jesus as your Saviour, He comes into your life. And when He comes in, He comes in with all His love. That love does some

wonderful things for us. It cleanses us from all our sins
and guilt. Did you know, Debbie, that the Bible says
that after we confess our sins to Him, He takes our sins
and casts them in the depths of the sea and remembers
them against us no more? Think of the worst sins
you've committed—and I mean all of them. After
you've asked the Lord to forgive them, He not only
forgives them; he doesn't even remember them!"

"You're kidding!" I responded. "I can hardly believe that!"

"But it's true, Debbie. That's what the Bible says,
and I believe it. But some people struggle with that
verse. Their friends—I imagine it would be their so-
called friends—still remember their sins. Even the
devil remembers your sins. And sometimes he'll remind you of them and try to place you under a terrible
bondage of guilt. But God never remembers them.
They're forgiven!"

I sure would like that to be true in my life, I thought.

"Would you like to experience Christ's love and
receive Jesus as your Saviour now?" Linda asked.

"Oh, yes! This is what I need and really want!"

She explained that to receive Christ, you confess
your sins to Him. You may not be able to remember
all of them, she said, but just include them in one big
statement. Just say, "Jesus, forgive me of all my sins."

Then she said I was to receive Christ in my heart by
faith. I didn't understand until she explained that the
Bible says Jesus stands at the door to a person's heart
knocking. If we just open up, He'll come in and live
within us.

Then she led me in a prayer that I repeated after
her. In it, in very simple faith, I asked Jesus to forgive

me of all my sins and invited Him to come and live in my heart.

When I got through, it all seemed too simple. I waited for some big emotional high. Nothing happened.

Linda must have anticipated my feelings and said, "Now, Debbie, according to your prayer, where is Jesus right now?"

I thought about it. I did ask Him to forgive my sins, and I did ask Him to come into my heart. I really meant what I had said, so I replied, "Jesus is now in my heart."

Linda slapped her knee. "That's it, Debbie! That's it! You have Jesus in your heart!"

"Okay," I said, "but why don't I feel any different?"

"People have all kinds of responses in receiving Jesus," she told me. "I mean, in some cases it's like lightning going off. People even jump up and down. But in most cases it doesn't happen that way. In fact, sometimes people don't feel very different. Others simply feel as though a great weight has been lifted from their shoulders."

She paused to be sure I was taking it all in.

"No matter how we feel," she went on, "the fact remains that Jesus lives within our hearts. He said so in the Bible, and we believe what He has said in His Word—not how we feel. He's in your heart right now because you invited Him to be there. And He will always be there. Continue to believe that, Debbie. That's where the faith comes in. Feeling will come after faith. Some people want to feel good first and then have faith. But that's not the Bible order. You need to have faith first; the feelings will come later. There will be a time when you will feel much better."

I sure hoped so, because right then I started feeling terribly nauseated. I tried to get up and head for the bathroom, but I merely got my head over the side of the bed and vomited all over the floor. What a stinking mess!

I guess Linda was right. I really needed the Lord, to go through what I was facing. Well, before I knew what had happened, my bowels cut loose, and I messed all over the bed.

Feeling terribly embarrassed and helpless as a child, I looked up at Linda. Would you believe she was still smiling—even in this horrible stench?

"Let me go get some paper and a mop," she said. "It looks like you just exploded."

I half expected her to yell at me because of what I had done. But she didn't. I think I would have if I had been in her place. This home really must be different.

In a few minutes she came back with tissues, a bucket, and a mop. She started on me first, washing me with a washcloth and drying me with a towel. Then she cleaned up the bed, changed the linens, and scrubbed up the floor.

As I lay there hardly able to move, I started to cry. I just couldn't get over the love of these people for an absolute stranger. First it was Mom B. and Randy. Now Linda. And the other staff too. It was just too much to believe.

Linda left to clean up the mops and buckets. And when she came back, she was still smiling! She must have that smile pasted on.

I feebly thanked her for all she had done and apologized for making such a mess. By now beads of sweat were pouring from my body, soaking the sheets.

"Hey, Debbie," Linda comforted, "you don't need

to apologize. We believe every girl who comes here is a gift from God. No matter what you look like, we still believe you are a gift."

Just then my stomach wrenched again. This time Linda grabbed the bucket and stuck it under my chin. I leaned over and retched and retched and retched. Oh, how I hurt! Linda rubbed my back and started praying.

Finally I fell back exhausted. *Can I take this?* I wondered. Maybe I should leave and go back to the street where I could get some heroin. I had never been this sick in all my life.

Linda wiped my sweaty brow and said, "Debbie, not only does Jesus save us, but He also has the power to heal us. I must admit that I don't understand everything about healing. Sometimes girls are healed during their kicking, and other times it doesn't happen. But I'm going to pray now and ask the Lord to heal you and take away this kicking. You try to believe with me."

I never had heard of such a thing before. Could Jesus heal too?

I was too sick to say anything, but I closed my eyes as Linda began to pray. Suddenly I became aware of great peace. It seemed to envelop my whole body. Oh, how good it felt!

The next thing I knew I woke up, and the room was full of light. Daytime? Was it possible? How could I possibly be kicking cold turkey and go to sleep? No one did that! But the last thing I remember was Linda praying for Jesus to heal me—

I sat up and looked around. I couldn't believe it! I felt so good. Then it hit me. I had been *healed!*

When I heard someone in the hallway, I called, "Hello, out there!"

The door opened, and there stood Mrs. Benton—smiling, as always. "Well, Debbie, what are you doing, sitting up?" she asked. "I heard you were pretty sick last night."

"Mom B., I can't believe it! I feel so good!"

She clapped her hands together, then threw her arms joyfully toward the ceiling. "Praise the Lord! Jesus healed you!"

I raised my hands too and yelled, "Praise the Lord! I'm healed."

Mom B. excitedly threw her arms around me, saying over and over again, "Isn't Jesus wonderful?"

I agreed wholeheartedly. Then I said, "I feel like getting up and getting dressed. I'm starved!"

"Great! Just great!" Mom B. responded. "I'll head down to the kitchen and fix something for you."

Her fix it? Wouldn't all the girls be eating breakfast now? That made me ask: "What time is it?"

"About three in the afternoon. You've had quite a sleep!"

I couldn't believe it. Jesus had healed me, and I had slept. He had healed my kicking! "Does this happen every day around here?" I asked Mom B.

"Well, I wouldn't say every day," she responded. "But there are times that the Lord does heal. And it is beautiful."

"I can sure agree with that," I said. "This is absolutely fantastic. I feel worlds better than I have in years. Not only am I physically well, but I think I'm beginning to feel like a Christian!"

That triggered her, and she came over and

squeezed me again. She seemed happier than I was—if that was possible.

Then she seated herself at the edge of my bed and started talking. "Debbie," she said, "God wants to do even greater things than this in your life. What you must do is determine to live for Him.

"I remember once my husband John and Terri Johnson went to pick up this girl in Brooklyn. She asked if my husband was the prophet John. Of course they laughed. My husband is no prophet.

"But what really had happened was that a girl came in here and was terribly sick, just like you were. As my husband prayed, Jesus healed her of her kicking."

She paused as she remembered the details of what I gathered must have been a hard story to tell.

"Then, Debbie," she went on, "a very sad thing happened. This girl, her name was Rachel, left our program after about a week. My husband had a special word from God for her as she walked out our front door. God told my husband that if Rachel wasn't careful, she would soon be dead.

"You see," she explained, "when Christ does something wonderful for us, we must be careful not to turn our backs on Him. Here God had done this great miracle for Rachel, and then she walked out of here. My husband warned her not to go, but she persisted."

"You mean that girl just walked out of here after the Lord had healed her?" I asked.

As Mom B. nodded, her eyes brimmed with tears. "So when Rachel got back to Brooklyn, she started telling everybody on the street that my husband had said she was going to die. She laughed about it; but, Debbie, one week later Rachel died of an overdose!"

"She did? She really died that soon?"

"Yes, that is exactly what happened. You see, God in His love and mercy was trying to warn Rachel through my husband. But Rachel didn't heed the warning."

I had no idea that God was that personally concerned about us. But I certainly wasn't going to question it—especially after what He had done for me last night.

"So after Rachel died," Mom B. continued, "people on the street remembered what my husband had said. So when he and Terri picked up this other girl in Brooklyn, she had heard about Rachel. That was the girl who thought my husband must be the prophet John!

"Now, of course, Brother B. is no prophet. But I just wanted to tell you that story. Debbie, never turn your back on the Lord. As soon as you do, God takes His hand off your life, and the devil takes over. Jesus has come to build up your life, but the devil will always try to destroy it. So stay on the Lord's side, and He will always watch out for you."

The moral of that story certainly wasn't lost on me. "Well, for sure I know where I'm going to stay," I told her. "I want to stay put. I want all that God has for me!"

She patted my back and said, "That's good, Debbie; that's real good. You're learning already."

When she walked out of the room, I looked for some clothes, and inside a drawer I found my clothes—all clean and fresh. Even getting dressed seemed like an adventure, and then I bounced down the stairs to the dining room. Mom B. had some soup and a sandwich waiting. Oh, it tasted so good!

As I ate, she sat across from me. "We'll have some

real good food for supper. I know you are going to enjoy our meals. In fact, all the girls cook the meals."

"You mean some of the young ones I've seen are cooks too?"

"They certainly are, and they do a really good job."

"Wow! I can't imagine a young girl in a kitchen."

"Well, Debbie, you never know where you'll end up. Maybe you'll be a cook."

I laughed. "Mom B., I couldn't cook water without burning it!"

She just smiled. "That's what a lot of our girls think. But when Jesus comes into their hearts, you would be amazed at the talents our girls discover they have. Not only do they do all the cooking, but they work outside in the yard. Some of them even drive the dump truck! They do the snowplowing and painting and all those kinds of things. Some work in the office as secretaries, and others clean the house. We don't have a large staff, so we depend on the girls, and they really come through for us. It's just marvelous the work they do.

"But, of course," she went on, "the main thing is the school. You'll go to school from eight in the morning until noon. It's called a School for Christian Growth. We teach our girls the principles of the Bible, making it relevant and practical. The Scriptures teach us how to live. And when we follow them, we find that abundant life Jesus talked about. What we try to do, Debbie, is to give you the tool—God's Word. Then when you graduate from the program and face the real world, you are equipped. God will use His Word to help you resist all temptation and become the person He wants you to be."

"Well, I certainly don't know much about the Bible," I said as I took another bite from the sandwich. "I've got a lot to learn."

"The Bible even talks about that," Mom B. said. "It calls new Christians 'babes in Christ.' Linda was telling me that last night you received Jesus as your Saviour. Now you're like a baby. We will share with you and teach you how to grow as a Christian—from being an infant to becoming a growing, mature person in Jesus. And you're going to be surprised, after you get to know God's Word, how much you'll be able to handle in life. The beautiful part, Debbie, is that the Lord has a beautiful plan for you, and I'm excited to see it take place in your life."

The intercom in the dining room buzzed, interrupting our conversation. Mom B. got up to answer. I really didn't hear what she said. I was too busy downing that delicious soup and sandwich. Then she called me and told me I had a telephone call. "We let our girls receive calls," she said, "but we like your friends to call on the pay phones. That way we won't tie up our business lines with personal calls. Tell them to call next time on 424-3685."

Who in the world would be calling me? Nobody knew I was here.

When I said, "Hello," a voice asked, "Is this Debbie Carter?"

I started to slam down the receiver. I knew that voice. It was my pimp, Harding Mason.

He screamed into the phone, "Debbie, I'm going to get you and get you good!"

How did Harding find out I was up here? And now what was I going to do? Jesus had made a big change in my life. I sure couldn't go back to Harding. But now that he knew where I was, I was sure he would try to kill me!

"Thought you were pretty smart to get away from me, didn't you?" he snarled. "Well, I'm smarter than you are. It didn't take me long to find out you had gone off with those two women. And some people on the streets knew they were from that home up there."

"Now, Harding, let me tell you something. I want you to hear me. I'm not the person I used to be. I have received Jesus as my Saviour. He's saved me and healed me. I'm born again now, Harding. The past is over with—for good!"

"Don't think you can get away from me!" Harding screamed. "I finally located George Turner, and you gave me a pack of lies. I don't like being made a fool of. You're a dirty, filthy liar—that's what you are. Don't give me none of this Christian bit. You're a creep, and I'm going to come and get you away from there!"

"Don't talk like that, Harding. These people up here are wonderful Christians, and . . . "

"Don't tell me what to do!" he exploded. "I'm coming up there with a loaded .45, and I'm going to blast your brains out right on the spot if you don't come back here with me. You understand?"

I pleaded with him. "Harding, you're the one who doesn't understand. I'm not the same Debbie you knew. I'm free! Absolutely free! I'm not a junkie! I'm not a prostitute! I'm a Christian! I've been saved, and my life is totally changed!"

"Don't try to talk religion to me!" Harding shouted. "I know right where that home is. I'm holding one of their brochures in my hands, and it tells how to get there. And I'm coming, Debbie. I'm coming to get you!" With that he slammed the receiver down.

I turned, and Mrs. Benton was sitting at the table. "What was that all about?" she asked.

"That was Harding Mason, my pimp. He knows where I am."

"Well, Debbie, I think you handled it just right. You told him it was all over. Now Jesus is going to give you new friends."

"But that's not all there is to it, Mom B.," I said. "He's headed up here with a loaded .45. If I don't go with him, he says he's going to blow my brains out right here!"

Mom B. was completely unruffled. "Only if the Lord allows it, my dear," she said. "Mr. Mason isn't fighting against you; he is fighting against the Lord. The Lord has put a hedge around you, Debbie. He has guardian angels watching you. I believe that."

"But Mom B., you don't know Harding. I mean, he's vicious. I really think he's a maniac."

Mom B. smiled again. "Jesus loves maniacs too."

"You mean Jesus loves Harding? I mean, Harding is so despicable that I can't put it in words! Does Jesus love him?"

She nodded. "It's hard to believe, but Jesus loves Harding."

I didn't feel like finishing the last few bites of my lunch, so Mom B. suggested, "Why don't we go down to the basement prayer room? The Lord has another experience for you. It's called the baptism in the Holy Spirit. I think you are going to need it."

In the prayer room Mom B. explained from the Bible about the baptism in the Holy Spirit. She said it was God's way of giving us great power: power to tell

others about Jesus, power to live above sin, and power
to speak to the Lord in worship and praise.

I certainly needed that power—especially when I
knew Harding was on his way to kill me.

Mom B. prayed with me, and I had the beautiful
experience of receiving the baptism in the Holy Spirit.
It was so wonderful kneeling there worshiping and
thanking the Lord. As I began to praise Him, He took
over my entire being. I was simply bubbling over with
love for my wonderful Saviour!

When we went back upstairs, supper was ready.
Mom B. introduced me to Theresa, my big sister. New
girls are always assigned a big sister when they first
come. The big sisters show them around the home and
go with them to their classes and assignments.
Theresa and I hit it off right away.

I waited apprehensively for Harding that evening,
but he didn't come. Afternoon the next day I was
sitting with Theresa on the back stairs of the home as
she explained about memorizing verses of Scripture.
Then a car drove up, and a man got out. My heart
jumped. Harding!

13 When I saw Harding, I ran inside as fast as I
could, screaming, "Mom B.! Mom B.!" I glanced back
toward the parking lot. Sure enough, Harding was
headed this way. I knew he had that .45 under his belt.
I couldn't go back with him, so that meant he would
kill me. What a waste—now that I was just learning
how to live!

Mom B. was nowhere around, so I ran through the

dining room toward the kitchen. Maybe I could get through the kitchen and into the basement. There ought to be a lot of hiding places down there!

I hit the kitchen door going full blast—and ran smack into Brother Benton. He was carrying a cup of coffee. The cup went straight up into the air, splattering coffee all over him and me, and he went sprawling across the kitchen floor. I did too, landing near his feet.

Brother B. quickly brushed the hot coffee off and said, "Well, Debbie, are you trying out for the football team? That was the best block I've seen in all my life. You knocked me clear across the kitchen floor!"

I jumped up and yelled, "I'm sorry about that, but I'm in serious trouble. I mean, it's all over for me!"

He slowly got to his feet. Nothing ever seemed to ruffle him.

"Now, Debbie, don't tell me the Russians have landed and we're about to be taken prisoner."

"Brother B., this is serious! My pimp just came walking in the front door with a loaded .45. He's out to get me!"

"Oh, isn't that just wonderful!" he responded. "Here's an opportunity to reach one of the hardest people in the world with the Gospel! Thank the Lord!"

"What?" I yelled incredulously. "Harding won't listen to any gospel. He's just full of hate and bitterness. And if you get in his way, he won't mind shooting you either!"

Brother B. smiled. "Now, now, Debbie, let's just calm down. I've encountered a few pimps in my life, and I'm still living. Some of them have wanted to kill me too. But the Lord has ways of turning these things around. Let's trust God."

I decided I could trust God easier when I was hidden in the basement. But when I turned to run, Brother B. grabbed my arm. "Whoa there, young lady. Let's go have a talk with your pimp."

I jerked away. "Brother B., I don't think you know how serious this is. Harding has threatened to kill me. He has beaten me and mutilated my body and even locked me in with hungry rats. Now he's after me, and I'm scared to death!"

Brother B. moved over and put his arm gently around my shoulder. "Debbie, I'm not making light of your pimp. I know about these dudes. Some are murderers, and some keep girls captive in terrible slavery. But let's believe that Harding's coming up here is a divine encounter—that God really wants to reach into Harding's life and save him. Maybe he's the worst. But that's all the more reason he needs to experience the love of Jesus!"

"But, Brother B., supposing he kills us!"

He smiled again. "Why wouldn't that be wonderful, Debbie? We'd be in heaven!"

Before I knew what was happening, Brother B. dragged me into the dining room and then into the living room. That's when I saw him, standing there, hands on hips. When he saw me, he screamed, "Debbie, I knew I would get you. Now are you going to come peacefully, or am I going to have to do this by force?"

Brother B. ignored the threat and stepped forward and stuck out his hand. "Harding," he said, "welcome to the Walter Hoving Home. We're so glad that you could come today."

Wow! That took some cool!

Harding was nonplussed. First he looked at Brother B.'s extended hand. Then he looked at me. And while Harding just stood there, Brother B. took another step forward, grabbed Harding's dangling hand, and shook it. "Harding, we're so glad you're a friend of Debbie," he said. "She was just telling me about you. And what a beautiful surprise this day to have you show up here on our property. I'm sure God has brought you here."

Harding blinked his eyes and mumbled, "Yeah, I guess it is quite a place. Didn't expect anything like this."

Still holding Harding's hand, Brother B. guided him to the dining room. "I was just attempting to have a cup of coffee," he said. "Why don't you sit down with me for a moment? I suppose that after that ride up from the city, you're ready for some coffee. Do you like it black or with cream?"

Harding was bewildered by this turn of events. "Uh, I like it with just a little cream. No sugar."

Brother B. turned to me. "Debbie, please get me another cup of coffee. This time I'd like to have it served at the table—not all over me." He laughed, and I giggled. But I still couldn't get away from the seriousness of the situation. At any moment Harding might whip out that .45 and start blasting away!

"Debbie, also please get a nice, hot cup of coffee for your good friend and mine, Harding Mason."

As I walked into the kitchen, I heard Brother B. say, "Come on over here, Harding; have a seat. Let me tell you about the tremendous things God has done for us in allowing us to get this beautiful estate. It's a miracle of the Lord!"

I closed the kitchen door behind me. Just ahead was

the door to the basement. Should I run down there and hide? Or should I run off the property? But what would happen then? No, I'd better stay around. If Brother B. was willing to put his life on the line, then I certainly should have half as much courage. So I got the two cups of coffee, put a little cream in one, and headed back to the dining room.

As I walked to the table and set down the cups, Brother B. suggested, "Debbie, please sit down with us. Let's share with Harding some of the fantastic things that have happened in your life since he last saw you."

I pulled out a chair across from Harding. I figured that way I could keep an eye on him. I could also see he was still angry.

Brother B. started in. "You know, Harding, there are so many things wrong in this world. Did you know that Christ really didn't intend it to be this way? I mean, you think of the terrible things that go on in Times Square—the filth and all the people who are not really living. They're just existing. I mean, their hearts are full of bitterness, hatred, and confusion, and really have nowhere to go. There is such hurt on these people's faces."

"Yeah, I know, man," Harding responded. "It's bad out there."

"You know, Harding," Brother B. continued, "every once in a while I'm down around Times Square, and I walk through those streets. Sometimes I look at those junkies and prostitutes and all of those other people, and I begin to cry. I've actually stood on the corner of Forty-second and Eighth and wept. I just want to gather all those people up and put them in my car and bring them up here and tell them how much

Jesus loves them. Oh, if they would just learn to trust Jesus as their Saviour, they would have a much better life."

Harding looked perplexed. "You mean, Reverend, you stood on the street corner crying for us, I mean, for those people?"

"At times I just can't help myself," Brother B. answered. "And when I think of the great things God has done for our girls for so many years now, I can't help but try to reach out to those who are still hurting in such a terrible way.

"You know, Harding, I remember when we brought Debbie up here a couple of days ago. She was picked up off the street in horrible condition—a junkie enslaved to heroin, a person who didn't have love and understanding when she was growing up and who ended up out on the streets. I guess you know what that's all about."

Harding nodded. "Yeah, man, it's terrible out there. I mean, it's dog-eat-dog. Lots of people get knifed or shot. And nobody is your friend. I mean, real mean, man."

"But you know," Brother B. interjected, "one time I was asked by a famous person why God allowed deplorable conditions like Times Square and the ghetto to exist. God really gave me the answer to that. You see, God didn't make those horrible conditions. God didn't make the junkie. God didn't make the prostitute. God didn't make those terrible rat-and-roach-infested tenements. It is because of evil that all those things exist. And Jesus died to make all the things that are wrong go right. In fact, Harding, if everybody on Forty-second Street would suddenly be born again, do you know what would happen to all those filthy triple-X-rated movies and porno shops?"

"No, what?"

"Why, nobody would go in there, and they'd go out of business. And did you know that if everybody on Forty-second Street got saved, you could walk down there any time of the day or night and not be mugged.

"Now if we spread that—Forty-second Street and all the people getting saved there—around the world, Harding, there would be no more murders, no more junkies, no more prostitutes, no more crime! Everybody in this whole wide world would live at peace with each other. That just gives you an idea of the tremendous impact Jesus wants to make upon this world. He wants to change it and get people loving each other."

I'd never thought of it that way before, but Brother B. sure was right. I glanced over at Harding, wondering how he was responding. He was staring down at his hands, then at the bulge on his right side. That's where he had his .45. Did Brother B. know it was there? What would happen if Harding pulled it out?

I didn't have long to wonder, because Harding was becoming more and more agitated. Then he reached down, and suddenly he had that gun aimed at us.

I leaped to my feet. Reverend Benton simply pulled me down again. "Debbie, stay cool!" he ordered. "God knows what He is doing!"

Harding shifted the aim of the gun from me to Brother B. and then back to me. He didn't seem to be sure whom he was after! Then he aimed it at Brother B. and said, "Reverend, you've been talking about power. Well, this is my power. This is how I rule my world. I do it by force."

"Harding," Brother B. responded, "what you say is probably true. But what does it bring you? Do you really have peace? Can you honestly say you're satisfied with the way you're living?"

There was a long pause. I was so nervous that my knees knocked together. Suppose Harding pulled that trigger. It was aimed right at Brother B.'s heart!

For the longest time nobody said anything. Then Brother B. said it again: "Do you really have peace?"

Harding slowly shook his head. "No, Reverend, I don't."

Well, just then Mom B. came bursting into the dining room. As soon as she saw the three of us sitting there, she called, "Oh, Debbie, is this your brother? Isn't it nice for you to have a visitor?"

When he heard her, Harding quickly moved the gun under the table. And before I could answer her, she had rushed over and put her arms around Harding. "Young man, what is your name?" she asked, adding, "You sure are handsome!"

Did she know he was my pimp and had a loaded .45 under the table? I was scared to death that she was going to try to hug him. But she didn't. She simply patted his shoulder.

"Mom B.," I said, this is a friend of mine, Harding Mason."

She put out her hand to shake his hand—the hand with the gun. "Oh, Harding, we are so glad to have you here," she said. "I thought maybe you were Debbie's brother. We're so glad you're here."

Just then I heard a thud. The gun! Harding then reached up to shake Mom B.'s hand, and she gave him one of her super smiles. "I was just on my way down to the basement cooler to check our food supply," she said. "Be sure to stay for supper. We'd love to have you."

With that she turned and walked away. Harding, once again perplexed by the turn of events, mumbled a few words of thanks.

The idea of Harding staying for supper was preposterous! The big question was whether or not I would be here for supper. Or would I even be alive?

Harding began looking underneath the table. Should I try to lunge for the gun before he did and get it away from him? If the gun was his power and I had the gun, then his power would be gone, and he would have to leave. Without me!

14 I had just decided to lunge to the floor for Harding's gun. But before I could do anything, Brother B. reached down and grabbed it. This was better yet. Now Brother B. could get Harding out of here—with Harding's own loaded pistol. What a turn of events! What a miracle!

When Brother B. raised up with the gun, Harding jumped up and backed over against the wall.

As Brother B. stood, I looked at him, dismayed. He had the gun, but, oh no! He had hold of the barrel! Didn't preachers know anything about guns?

Never in a million years was I ready for what happened next. Brother B. extended the handle of the gun toward Harding and said, "Here's your gun, Harding. I guess you dropped it."

Then Brother B. cut loose with that infectious laugh of his. Harding looked at the gun, at me, at Brother B. back at the gun, and slowly raised his hand to accept the pistol. He was obviously shaken by this turn of events.

"Don't you know, Reverend," he said, "that that gun is loaded?"

Brother B. laughed again. "I sure hope so, Harding. If you ever have to use it, you'd look awfully silly shooting with an empty gun. That wouldn't do you any good at all!"

Totally bewildered now, Harding stood there just studying the gun in the palm of his hand. I knew it had to be the first time in his life anybody had ever done anything like this to him!

"Let's sit back down and finish our coffee," Brother B. suggested. "You'll just have to excuse my wife. She doesn't have a mean bone in her body. Everybody is her friend. Now if I told her who you really are, it wouldn't make any difference. She'd love you just the same."

Harding tucked the .45 back into his belt and moved back to the table. "Man, I just can't get over this," he said, shaking his head. "You people certainly are different, aren't you?"

I smiled for the first time as I said, "Harding, it's so different up here. I mean, the peace of Jesus is so strong that it affects everybody who comes!"

"So that's what you call it," Harding responded. "I will have to admit that as I walked in that front door a few minutes ago, something strange happened to me. I don't know what you know about me, Reverend, but Debbie used to work for me. I know I wasn't good to her, but I had to make money to live. I grew up in the ghetto and had nothing; but when I went to using girls, I had everything. And one of the things that sends me up the wall is to have a girl try to cut out on me. That's what Debbie did. I came up here to get her back. When I walked across your parking lot, I decided that nobody was going to stand in my way. I'd kill if I had to, to get her back. But as I walked through your front door, all that hatred and bitterness started to drain out of me. Suddenly I just couldn't do what I wanted to do. I felt I had better get out of this place. Yet I wanted to stay."

Brother B. smiled—this time a great big one. "Harding, that was the presence of Christ that is so strong in this place. You see, Jesus is very real. He's become real to Debbie. She has given her heart to the Lord and is determined to live for Him, come what may. Not because she has to, but because she wants to. You know the bitterness and hatred that used to be in Debbie's life. Now they're gone. Jesus took all those things out and replaced them with His wonderful love. And let me tell you, Harding, it's for real."

Harding sat there staring at his coffee cup. No one said anything, but I noticed his hands trembling. I glanced at Brother B. His lips were moving in prayer. Then I saw a great big tear trickle down Harding's cheek. I couldn't believe that that good-for-nothing pimp was crying. I'd never seen any sign of tenderness in him ever before!

Harding's tears turned to sobs, and before long all three of us were crying together. Brother B. pushed back from the table and came around and put his arm around Harding. "Do you know you came here today by the divine act of the Lord?" he asked. "I know you think you came to get Debbie, but the Lord had other reasons for it. He had you come here so He could reveal Himself to you—so you could get acquainted with a power greater than your .45. And let me tell you, Harding, if at this minute you give your life to Jesus, things are going to be so different. I mean, so different. A peace like you've never known will be yours. There will be a sparkle in your eyes. People will know you're different!"

Harding slowly raised his head and turned to look at Brother B. "Reverend," he said, "you don't know very much about me. I've been so terribly mean and have done such unbelievably evil things. I don't deserve the peace you're talking about. I am full of evil!"

Harding began to sob again—this time like a child. So help me, I could never believe this would ever happen to Harding!

"I know how you must feel," Brother B. sympathized, "but that's the beautiful part of it. We don't receive Christ because we *deserve* Him. We receive Christ because we *need* Him. And you certainly need Him."

"Yes," Harding responded, "I certainly need Him. Do you think He will take me, wicked as I am?"

"Harding, I *know* He will take you. Right now, right here in this dining room, you can receive Jesus as your Saviour."

I had already learned that about the Lord: He always meets you where you are!

"Harding, would you like to receive Jesus as your Saviour now?"

An obvious battle was raging for Harding's soul. The forces of evil were lined up against the love of Christ. And I was praying that this evil pimp would be born again.

Brother B. repeated the question, and Harding finally said, "Yes, I would like to receive Him."

"Debbie, please go to my office and get my Bible,"

Brother B. said. "I want to show Harding, from the Scripture, how to be saved."

I leaped from my chair and ran into the kitchen yelling, "Praise the Lord! Praise the Lord!" Just then Mom B. came out of the basement and demanded, "What's happened?"

I threw my arms around her and announced, "Harding wants to be saved!"

"Oh, glory to God! Thank You, Jesus!" she shouted as she jumped up and down all over that kitchen. We were having such a good time praising God that I almost forgot what I was supposed to do. After all, we didn't have Harding saved yet!

It didn't take me long to find the Bible and bring it back to Brother B. Then I turned back to the kitchen, still shedding tears of joy over this strange turn of events. I wanted Brother B. and Harding to be alone as they talked.

Mom B. and I had a cup of coffee in the kitchen while we waited for news from the dining room. Finally I heard some stirring around in there, and I couldn't wait any longer. Both men were standing by the table. When Harding saw me, he smiled and said, "Debbie, I'm now your Christian brother in the Lord. Could I give you a brotherly hug?"

I looked at Brother B. to see if it was okay. He was standing there smiling. So Harding stepped forward and threw his arms around me, weeping. "Debbie," he said, and I knew his heart was breaking, "you're the first one I must ask to forgive me. I don't deserve any of what has happened to me today. I really deserve to die. But God has forgiven my sins. And, Debbie, would you please forgive me for all the horrible, wicked things I have done to you—for the ways I have humiliated you and abused you. Oh, how I wish I could turn back the clock and change all those things. But I can't. Would it be possible for you ever to forgive me?"

I drew back just a little and looked into his pleading eyes. "I sure do forgive you, Harding," I said. "God has forgiven me for all the horrible, evil things I've done, so I certainly can forgive you for what you've done to me. And Harding, let's thank God that out of those terrible things, our evil past has led us both to Christ!"

By this time Mom B. was in the dining room hugging Harding and me. Then the other girls started to come in. Word had gotten around about the drama being played out in the dining room, and they had been praying all over the place. I introduced Harding as a Christian Brother in the Lord. It was super!

Well, Harding really did stay for supper. Then Brother B. was able to arrange to get Harding into the Teen Challenge program. Brother B. said they had learned it was important to get new converts out of their old environment until they could be grounded in God's Word. Teen Challenge did for boys what the Walter Hoving Home did for girls.

My year at the home was such a beautiful experience. God taught me so many things from the Bible. Then I went on to Evangel College in Springfield, Missouri, where I majored in communications. I felt I needed to know how to use the media to tell others about Jesus and what He could do for them.

After three years at Evangel College, I decided to spend a summer working at the Walter Hoving Home. I filled in for some of the staff while they had their vacations. I felt it was important to give a little bit of

my life to something that had done so much for me.
And it really was the only home I had.

One Saturday night some of us decided to go down
to Times Square to do some witnessing and distribute
tracts. Of course, I had mixed emotions about going
back to the pit from which the Lord had rescued me.
But I was also anxious to share with the girls on the
streets how Christ loved them—just as Randy had
done for me.

I talked with some girls I had known in my old life.
What shocked me were the number who were now
dead!

About twelve of us were witnessing on the street
that night. It was about eleven o'clock when one of our
girls came up and said, "Debbie, you just have to come
down here and listen to this guy preaching. He's with
a group of four fellows. He says he used to live in this
area, and, boy, is he ever socking it to them!"

She had me by the arm and dragged me toward the
corner where quite a crowd had gathered. Whoever
was speaking certainly had a commanding voice. I
stood at the edge of the crowd thanking the Lord for
this witness. I couldn't see the guy who was talking,
but I could certainly agree with what he was saying. He
told about how he used to walk these same streets lost
and alone and hurt. He said he was mean and evil. I
wondered if he had been here when I was. So I kind
of pushed my way through the crowd. When I got to
where I could see him, I couldn't believe my eyes. It
was Harding Mason!

I wanted to rush forward and throw my arms around
him, but I knew that would be bad timing. Right now
he needed to get across the message of Christ's love.

Harding was going on: "Folks, I was the meanest,

most evil pimp here on the street. I made my girls
slaves. I beat them and did every imaginable thing to
make them work for me. I was the filthiest of the filthy.
But Jesus Christ came into my life and changed all
that. Now I have a spring to my step and a sparkle in
my eye. And I have the joy of living for Christ within
my heart. And it can be just as real for you too!"

He paused as he looked out over the crowd. "And
now, friends, I have a little surprise for you," he said.
"I just noticed that standing here in the midst of all of
us is one of the girls who used to work for me. She,
too, has a dramatic story to tell. Friends, I'd like you
to meet a friend of mine and a special friend of Jesus.
Her name is Debbie."

I couldn't believe it! Harding was introducing me to
all these people! I hurried to where he was standing.
First he stuck out his hand to shake. Then he threw his
arms around me. "Debbie, I hope you don't mind my
asking you to speak. It's been four years since I saw
you that wonderful day at the home, but I just felt you
would have something to share with these people.
Some fellows are up from our school witnessing on the
street. Want to tell the people about Jesus?"

Did I! I hugged Harding and said, "I'm honored.
What a wonderful opportunity."

For a few moments I stood there sharing with those
people how Christ had wonderfully changed my life.
As I stood there looking into the eyes of all those
hurting people, I couldn't help but reach out to them
in love. I once had hurt with the same hurts, but for
me it was so different now. And I told them it could
be different for them too.

Harding stepped forward and gave an invitation for
those who wanted to receive Jesus as their Saviour. I

could hear weeping coming from all sides of that crowd, and about forty people raised their hands to receive Jesus. Afterward Harding got them all to one side and explained from his Bible how to be saved. It made me think of when Brother B. had done that for Harding. Now Harding was doing the same thing for others. What a beautiful continuation of God's plan for taking the message to the world!

Then he and his friends gave the people some literature provided by Glad Tidings Tabernacle on Thirty-third Street. He encouraged them to go there and learn how to live as Christians.

When he got through talking to those people, he came over to see me. I learned that he and the other fellows were all attending South-Eastern College in Lakeland, Florida, studying for the ministry. Well, we invited the fellows to come up to the home the next day and to speak for our chapel. They were glad to do that. I felt so proud as I heard Harding preach again. God really had placed a strong anointing on that young man's life.

The following day Harding had to leave for Florida again, and within a few days I headed back to Springfield, Missouri, and my senior year at Evangel College.

Well, Harding and I kept in touch by correspondence. Our letters became more and more frequent, and the subject of love became stronger. He'd even call me sometimes.

Harding graduated from South-Eastern a few days before I graduated from Evangel. A year later the most wonderful thing, outside of meeting Jesus, happened to me. I met Harding at a church altar, and I became Mrs. Harding Mason.

Harding and I live in Houston, Texas, now. God has

blessed our marriage with two beautiful boys. Harding is such a wonderful husband and father. And he is also the pastor of a growing church.

I can't get over how God is using him. Our church is full, and we have an active youth group. The people at our church know about our past. Harding and I are ashamed of the things we used to do and the way we used to live. But we're certainly not ashamed of what Jesus has done for us. It's our privilege to share His miracle of love with others and to help keep young people from making the same mistakes we made.

And what about you?

Do you know Jesus as your Saviour? You may never have been a pimp or a prostitute like we were. Maybe you haven't been dragged through the filthy gutters of sin the way Harding and I were. But still you have something in common with us: Down deep within your heart you may lack peace and joy—just as we did.

The reason you lack peace is that there is an empty void in a person's heart. That void cannot be filled by drugs. It cannot be filled by possessions. It cannot be filled by fame and fortune and attention and sex. It can only be filled by a Person—one Person—Jesus Christ.

Harding and I found that out and accepted Jesus as our Saviour. And it made an unbelievable difference for us.

It can for you too. You can accept Jesus right now. Remember, it doesn't matter where you are as you're reading my story. We don't necessarily go to Christ, but Christ comes to us. Right where we are!

Why don't you open your heart to Him right now? He wants to forgive all your sins and give you peace.

It's up to you. I pray you'll make the right decision and give your life over to Jesus. You'll never be sorry.

And you'll find the forgiveness, love, hope, and real purpose for living that you've been searching for.

I know you will. Because I did. And because Jesus' promise is for you too. He loved you so much that He died—just for you! And He lives so you, too, can have abundant life!

TA